THE CRYSTAL VOID

ILLUSTRATED EDITION

ALSO BY JOHN HOULIHAN

The Seraph Chronicles
The Trellborg Monstrosities
The Crystal Void
Tomb of the Aeons
Before The Flood
The Seraph Chronicles Volume One: Tales of the White Witchman

Mon Dieu Cthulhu! The Dubois Escapades
The Crystal Void Illustrated Edition
Feast of the Dead
Shadow of the Serpent
Keeper of the Hidden Flame (coming soon)

OTHER WORKS

Tom or the Peepers' and Voyeurs' Handbook
The Cricket Dictionary
Dark Tales from the Secret War (as editor)
The Constellation of Alarion (science fiction short stories)

THE CRYSTAL VOID
(ILLUSTRATED EDITION)
The first Mon Dieu Cthulhu! adventure

by John Houlihan

Cover Illustration is by Dimitri Martin
Design and Layout by Richard Gale and Tom Hutchings
Logo and illustrations by Mike Poole

CONTENTS

John Houlihan is a novelist and short story writer publishing over ten books including The Seraph Chronicles and Mon Dieu Cthulhu! series, *The Cricket Dictionary* and the BSFA-award nominated *The Constellation of Alarion*. He has also appeared in numerous sci-fi and fantasy short story collections including Signals, Near Future Fictions, When Shadows Creep, Corridors, Forgotten Sidekicks, Musketeers vs Cthulhu and many more.

He currently works for Modiphius Entertainment as an ENNIE-award winning game designer, creative lead and narrative director and works for many other TTRPG companies including Wizards of the Coast, Need Games and Monolith. He was also editor-in-chief of *Dragon+*. Before that he was a journalist and broadcaster for over thirty years, working in news, sport and especially videogames. He worked for *The Times*, *Sunday Times* and *Cricinfo* and is the former editor-in-chief of *Computer and Video Games.com*. He still works as a video game consultant and script writer.

Away from the written word he has an unnatural fondness for cricket, football, snowboarding, cycling, music, playing guitar and all forms of sci-fi, fantasy and horror. He has an unnatural dread about writing about himself in the third person and currently lives in his home town of Watford in the UK, because, well frankly, someone has to.

Find him at www.john-houlihan.net and @johnh259 on X.com

SPECIAL THANKS

With a tip of the Shako to ACD and GMF.

ONE

A Cognac for the Lieutenant Colonel

'Oh, ver' well if you insist *Monsieur*, Dubois will have a cognac to accompany this modest *vin rouge*. A large one? *Mais oui*, you are most kind, he 'as always said you British were the most generous of friends, as well as the most gallant of enemies. That is better, the spirit warms *l'esprit non?* These weary old bones welcome some succour from the chill of winter and the ravages of time.

So, Dubois raises his glass to you *Monsieur* but he will also raise it to him, the first Empereur, my beloved master, our little Corsican corporal who led us on *le grande* adventure all those years ago on the paths of glory and honour. He made Europe tremble before him and they both loved and feared us too, his *Grande Armée,* before your *Fer Duc* stopped him on that terrible day Dubois will not name.

They say little Louis-Napoléon, who seized the throne last year, has something of his uncle's genius about him. Dubois hopes he has, for these have been sad days for *la belle France*. We must hope for better times again.

Another? Well you are too kind Monsieur and an old soldier thanks you, though his doctor perhaps would not. Ach, what do these *toubib's* know? What is *la vie* if not for the living? Dubois would sooner die in his cups than in his sleep, since now a death on the field of glory is no longer possible.

Lieutenant Colonel Gaston Dubois (retired), at your service Monsieur, though alas, he is now of service to so few, though if the widow relents a little, perhaps we shall see if there is still a fire in the hearth and time for one last charge, *non*?! Hah! This cognac does Dubois good and takes him back to those old days when he was a *beau sabreur* – and not a fair face or a pair of lips from Madrid to Lisbon was safe from the twirling moustaches or the flashing blade of Dubois.

Ah, so it is him you wish to know of? Ah, well, there lies a tale and now, a shadow seems to pass across the fire and even forty odd winters later it is enough to make these old bones shudder. You see the *cheveux* upon my head? Well, that was the time when it first began to turn, from a deep chestnut, to the purest *blanc*.

And yet another? Hm, we may as well 'ave the bottle with your permission? *Bonne*, Pierre! Bring another glass for the kind Monsieur. You will wish to fortify yourself *mon ami* for this is as *sinistre* a tale as ever was told and before Dubois has finished, your hair may well be turned as white as his own. You have been warned, yet still you wish to proceed? *Bonne*, but *prudence* Monsieur and Dubois trusts this cognac will loosen his poor remembrance of your fair tongue, which he considers second only to the beauteous *Francais* itself.

It began in the autumn of 1810. That rascal Wellington… pardon Monsieur, old habits die hard. Any 'ow, le *Fer Duc* had finally given battle to our own dear child of victory Masséna and we had traded 'ow you say fisticuffs at Côa. Pff, Dubois remembers our brave *Chasseurs de la Siège* died in their droves as they pushed Black Bob's rascals across the river and once we 'ad him on the run, we began our long struggle through the mountains of Portugal to try and bring the matter to a satisfactory conclusion.

Oui, for in those days we still thought we could conquer the whole of the peninsula and even though he had given us a bloody nose at Bussaco, *le Duc* was forced to retreat into the heart of *Portugal* and dear Masséna pursued him with all 'aste. Dubois will not lie to you, it was an 'ard road Monsieur, as hard as a Jesuit's heart. *Les Portugais* – the Portuguese – had stripped the land bare as a skeleton's bleached bones and we suffered as we chased the British down country, until they eluded us and skulked behind those accursed earthworks at Torres Verdras. Is this the behaviour of gentlemen? *Non*, but *le Duc* would not stir himself from behind his defences to come and give battle and his cunning preparations meant we could not prise him from his 'ole.

'We danced and laughed and fell into each other's 'earts'

Yet we 'ussars bore it with the fortitude, providence and manliness you would expect of the premier chasseurs of *Le Armie Iberian*. We of the celebrated 13th Death's Head Hussars bided our time there, ever willing to patrol, probe and reconnoitre 'is lines and there were several minor affairs, when the more sporting of the English were willing to engage in a little light sword work. Ah, but they were magnificent days when Dubois thinks of them now, Monsieur, our brave and noble fellows with their *cadenettes* flying in the breeze, blades drawn as the bugle summoned us to the charge. The smell of *les chevaux*, the clash of steel, brave men trading strokes on the field of honour. Ah, it does this ruptured heart fair good to think of it.

Naturellement there were occasional amusements still to be 'ad away from the field and it was at one of these affairs – a ball organised by the regiment to raise *les esprits* – that Dubois first encountered *la belle* Odette. Oh Monsieur, words are simply not *adéquat* to describe her then in the dawn of her beauty. Dubois can still remember the first time he saw her as if it were this morning. Such poise, such elegance, the figure of a Venus, the face of an angel, such eyes, such lips, as if a very goddess had deigned to descend and walk upon this mortal plane. Forgive the moistness which invades Dubois' cheeks Monsieur, allow him a moment to gather himself and continue.

She wore the plainest of gowns and was quite unadorned save at her throat, where she wore a necklace of smoky gems. Yet these were mere trinkets, adjuncts to her beauty and Dubois was immediately enraptured, smitten as you say, *non?* He knew she must be his and she knew it too, for there were none so bold and dashing as the men of the 13th and of those – despite the poor shade you see before you here today – none so handsome, urbane or passionate as Dubois!

Cœur défaillir jamais gagné beau visage or how you say 'faint 'eart never won fair face'. In those days thought became deed for Dubois and he immediately paid his respects, extended his hand, swept her into his arms and onto the dance floor and for the rest of the night, the ball faded around us as we danced and laughed and fell into each other's 'earts.

As for my fellow officers? They were of no account and none dared to interrupt us, for one flash of Dubois' eyes and a bristle of his moustaches was enough to dismiss any such imagined impertinences. The fair Odette was the daughter of Colonel d'Hiver of the Guards but was also a true daughter of France and we were such kindred souls, it seemed as if we had known each other for years. Ah, Monsieur, they say love is sometimes to be found at first sight, but Dubois would not have believed such an assertion until that very night. You will gauge his seriousness when he tells you that – no matter how many tender female 'earts it broke – he took an oath to immediately forswore all others for his new love.

But even such star crossed lovers must eventually seek respite from the giddy whirl of the dancefloor and with aching feet but joyous hearts Dubois escorted his love to a cosy niche, while he fetched some refreshments. He returned *tout de suite* only to find his love receiving the unwanted attentions of a most strange looking fellow. He was a *Portugais*, that Dubois could see immediately, which may surprise you, but by no means was the whole country set against us in those days and some of the local gentry rather welcomed the enlightenment and refinements we Frenchmen brought to their rather unsophisticated land.

Even those *Portugais* who opposed us, while a little unschooled and perhaps overly prone to retreat, were nonetheless brave opponents when they stood in milor' Wellington's ranks and would perhaps only run away one time in every two. Yet this one wore no uniform and was not even a military man yet he had the affront to engage Dubois' love in idle flirtation? *Merde*! It would not do, Monsieur! As for my love, she was plainly distressed by his ungallant attentions, but brave girl that she was, was making a formidable show of hiding it, fluttering her eyelashes with clear disgust from behind her fan, while he peered down his nose at her through his eye glass.

'Monsieur,' Dubois said clicking his heels and allowing the fellow to turn and drink in his full formidable figure and manly bearing. 'I see you have made the acquaintance of the most beautiful woman in the world. A word of caution though, her beauty is liable to singe those who are not accustomed to its intense flame.' The scoundrel raised an eyebrow, looked Dubois up and down 'aughtily through his eye glass and Dubois took an instant dislike to the fellow.

He was handsome in a rather obvious kind of way, with the rich, well cut clothes and supercilious bearing of a natural aristo and he wore his foppish rags with a certain élan. The fellow was dark haired but his skin was curiously pale compared to the olive hues of his countrymen and he bore the frivolous chin beard these *Portugais* nobles sometimes affect. The mouth was full and sensual suggesting a debased nature, but it was his eyes that were most disturbing, dark and round, almost unnaturally so and they seemed to peer from that *visage* with an expression like a gutted 'alibut. Noble he may 'ave been but Dubois could see he was no gentlemen and he knew at once that our blades must cross, if not now, then in time. If he could have known what was to come to pass, Dubois would have drawn his blade and struck him down on the spot – without 'esitation. *Tres fort*–most strongly!

'I am the Marquis Phillipe de Figueira da Foz.' He gave the most derisory of nods.

'Lieutenant Gaston Dubois of the 13th.'

'Well, despite your lack of delicacy, I cannot fault your eyesight, Lieutenant. Mademoiselle d'Hiver is indeed a most charming young lady. Yet I also offer you a word of caution, or perhaps advice. Beware, for the sea cools even the most ardent of heat and this country has an inconvenient habit of separating even the most devoted of lovers.'

'Indeed? Such a forced separation could only come at the cost of my life, Monsieur Le Marquis.' Dubois reposted.

'Why, naturally,' he said and with that, the vile fellow turned on his 'eel and was soon lost amongst the milling throng. What an ill-mannered aristo rogue, Dubois should have punished him for his impertinence with an invitation to cross swords on the field of honour that very dawn. Although he knew Odette had merely been feigning politeness to this creature, it was only out of Dubois' consideration for his hosts and the Marquis' rapid exit that spared the fellow. Yet Dubois must confess that at that moment, a shadow crossed his heart which was not so easily dismissed.

Yet Dubois' misgivings eventually evaporated as the rest of the night passed in a giddy whirl of champagne and dancing and laughter and the first 'ints of dawn were lighting the sky when he escorted his beloved Odette back to the quarters of her father, Colonel d'Hiver. Few words were said at our parting, none were necessary in the passion of our embrace, yet somehow Dubois already knew an understanding had been made between us. He skipped back to his billet born on the very morning zephyrs themselves, certain, truly, that he had met the love of his life, *vous comprenez*–you understand?

Exhilarated but exhausted Dubois repaired to his quarters where he gratefully surrendered to the arms of Morpheus. He slept for most of the next day and when he awoke in the late afternoon, his head was still foggy and vague from the excesses of the night before. Yet while his mind was clouded, his heart was soaring and after he 'ad hunted up a morsel of breakfast and a vat of *café noir*, Dubois was once again restored to his former self. The rest of the afternoon was spent lounging around in the mess with his comrades and despite their boastful tales of gallantry and conquest, it was he who wore a secret smile which concealed his glowing 'eart.

As dusk became evening, Dubois sauntered across to the stables to visit his two mares, Rosalind and Eleanor to deliver some *pommes* to his other sweethearts. They munched them gratefully, snickering and whinnying their delight. Dubois smoked a thoughtful cheroot in the starlight and he was just strolling back to the mess ready to seek a little light supper, with Odette on his mind and love in his heart, when out of the shadows, a figure emerged.

'Monster! What 'ave you done with her?'

His sword was at once at Dubois' throat and his steel shivered and trembled, though whether through weakness or fury Dubois could not tell. Yet the point danced most alarmingly beneath his eyes.

'Calm yourself, sir, then explain. What is this dreadful thing of which you accuse Dubois?'

'Monster! The allure of her jewels was too much, was it not? Where is she? Speak or I will drive this point through your heart, so help me, *Mon Dieu!*

'Monsieur,# I said, calm as the surface of a lake in summer. 'I can assure you I know nothing of the matter to which you refer. If you speak of Mademoiselle d'Hiver...'

'I do.'

'Then I will trouble you not to bandy the name of *mon amour* with such reckle...' His words were like honey, but all the while Dubois had subtly been manoeuvring his assailant and in that moment his own sabre flashed, sparking against his blade and knocking it aside. Dubois sprang back onto the balls of his feet, ready to deliver a fierce blow to his foe, but now that he had a full view of his opponent, he stayed his hand.

'Colonel d'Hiver?!' For indeed it was the distinguished father of his love. Yet this was not the noble visage of the colonel of infantry who had led charge after charge into battle, but a pale shade of his former self. Monsieur le Colonel's face was distraught and his blade fell uselessly to the floor.

'Dubois. Tell me you have her, I will forgive any stain, any dishonour, if I know she is safe.'

'Slowly Colonel, slowly. I have not seen Odette since dawn when I walked her back to your quarters and saw her safely inside. I have been asleep or in the mess all day. *Mon Dieu*, what has 'appened?'

'She is missing from her bed and I thought it must be you who had stolen her away. Now her *maman* is gone, she is all I have, my dear sweet child, but she is a *naïf*, so pure, so innocent, that I believed she must have sought you out, or you her.'

'Believe me *mon* Colonel, I feel the same way, but to take her? *Non.* That is not the action of an honourable man and no way to win her heart or your affections. As for her gems? I care not two figs for them, they are nothing to me.'

'Forgive me, Dubois, I see I was wrong. An old man's concern for his sweet daughter has clouded his judgement. That necklace is a rare, curious piece that has been in our family for generations… I thought…'

'Perhaps it has, but it is a mere bauble compared to your daughter's beauty. Would you consider such a trinket reason enough to abduct her?'

'I can see now I have ascribed the basest of motives to you with little justification, Dubois. Forgive me if you can, for she is so precious to me, that it has driven me into gravely insulting you.'

'*L'amour d'un père est un puissant chose Mon Colonel* - the love of a father is a potent thing *mon* Colonel. As far as I am concerned there is nothing to forgive.'

'Yet, if she is not here with you, where is she? Her room is empty with no sign of disturbance and the necklace is also gone. You see how I might have leapt to this conclusion?'

'Do not give it another thought *mon* Colonel, but clearly there is some dastardly work afoot, and I believe I know its author.'

'You do? Speak *mon brave*, speak!'

'It is that villain, the Marquis da Foz.'

'The *Portugais* noble? But 'ow? Why?'

'His lurid attentions were directed at Odette last night before I intervened. Believe me, there is little accounting for the actions of these degenerate aristos, they are always eager to acquire more coin. If there is foul work here, I have no hesitation in laying it at 'is door. I will wager he abducted her and 'elped himself to her jewellery at the same time.'

'The swine, I will cut his heart out!'

'*Non, mon* Colonel, with the greatest respect, this is an assignment for a younger man and none will undertake it more gladly than Dubois. Give me a moment to saddle Rosalind and we will away to your quarters to see what we may see.'

A short while later we cantered to an 'alt outside the farmhouse where the Colonel and Odette had been billeted. His regiment of guards were camped outside, tall, strapping fellows who had swept all before them on the battlefields of Europe, but d'Hiver had sworn Dubois to secrecy lest further scandal arise and avoiding the picquets, we entered as quietly as field mice.

A quick examination of the scene of this outrage soon told Dubois the full story and he did not permit himself to show the fear or anger that stirred inside, lest it infect that brave old warrior. The Colonel, while an admirable man in many ways, had never hunted in the forests of the Ardennes where Dubois had spent his youth tracking wild beast and fowl. It did not take him long to discern what had happened at the scene of the crime.

The fiend and his helpers (for it was evident from the faint tracks below the window that he was not alone) had lured Odette into opening the downstairs window (perhaps impersonating Dubois 'imself no less!) and snatched her away from there. Strange, that this activity should have gone unnoticed in the middle of an armed camp, yet Da Foz was a devious scoundrel and undoubtedly knew the ground better than we and he had no doubt enjoyed some form of 'ome advantage.

Quickly, Dubois checked his kit and weapons and made sure he had enough spare ball and powder. Then he sprang upon his trusty mare and was reassuring d'Hiver with a confidence he perhaps did not entirely feel.

'Never fear, sir, I will bring her back to you and make sure that *salaud* pays for his infamy with his life!'

A father's eyes implored Dubois and not a word more did he need to speak. So, with a light touch of his spurs on Rosalind's flanks Dubois was soon off the night. The moon hung heavy and gibbous in the sky and even on horseback, it was not difficult to follow their footprints to where they had concealed their mounts a small distance away. They evidently knew their business well, for they rode in single file to conceal their numbers and the tracks disappeared away to the west toward the coast. Dubois set his little mare's nose to that point of the compass and followed as fast as Rosalind's sturdy legs could carry us.

Mon Dieu but it was an 'ard road my friend, for while they were easy enough for a seasoned huntsman to follow on the plain, the tracks soon led toward higher, stonier ground where even Dubois' *faucon's* eye was tested. But fortune favours the bold and just like your English fox'ounds on the scent, Dubois would not abandon his pursuit, for just the thought of his beloved in that fiend's arms, spurred him on and lent his Rosalind wings.

TWO

A Dance in the Moonlight

On and on Dubois rode and as he trotted into a small clearing, the sounds and scents of the night time forest seemed to diminish. Rosalind gave a snort and whinny as if she sensed something too and then, there he was, that grinning degenerate Da Foz, with Odette bound and slung across his saddle bow! Dubois' whiskers fair bristled with indignation and his sabre hissed from its sheath, but he just gave a contemptuous snort, disdaining even to draw his own blade.

'So, you are a brave man *and* a fool, Dubois. Better you had never walked this road.'

'An 'ussar does not walk, he rides!'

With that Dubois put spurs to Rosalind's flanks and charged the fiend point first, ready to slash those words from his throat, but the villain had prepared well and his ruffians came pouring from the trees in a devastating counter-charge. Dubois hacked at one, slashed at another's arms, but they were too many and cunningly they had placed their horses between us as a buffer, with no thought for their poor creatures' health. More of his villains assailed Dubois on foot and desperate, he forced Rosalind to dance and rear. Her hooves lashed out at another, there was a crack as his skull burst and he fell. But now their blows began to tell and as Dubois whirled Rosalind around again, a club buffeted his ribs, a blade raked his pelisse, his sabre was swept from his hand and he was dragged to the ground with blows raining down upon his Busby. *C'est vrai* – it is true he thought his last moment on earth 'ad come—but it 'ad not.

'More of his villains assailed Dubois on foot and desperate, he forced Rosalind to dance and rear.'

'Enough!' The blows ceased and Dubois was dragged to his feet, held in the iron grip of Da Foz's thugs.

'Such a brave man does not deserve to die... so quickly,' said the fiend. 'At least not before he has had a chance to hear a last goodbye from his love. Say your farewells my dear, for you will not look upon his face again.'

Odette's imploring eyes met Dubois' own and he held her gaze as he cursed Da Foz to the high heavens, rounding it off with an earnest lover's promise.

'…and if you sully her I will …'

'Enough! Continue and I will cut out your tongue as well. Yet, brave fool that you are, you should know, it was not Odette that I sought, though I will take her virtue nonetheless.'

'Make sure of me now Da Foz, for if not, I will 'unt you down…'

'Oh you'll die Dubois, be certain of that. But a Marquis of the blood does not sully his hands with such *common* toil. My men, on the other hand, have no such qualms. Fernando, I leave the details to you, but dispatch him in a manner worthy of your vile imagination. Make it both lingering and painful.'

Then he was gone and Dubois fought and shouted at the sound of retreating hooves but to little avail and soon he was trussed like a turkey at a country market. Even his poor Rosalind was subdued and hobbled and she looked at him with doleful eyes, while Da Foz's thugs debated in their debased way, the best method of dispatching poor Dubois. They casually discussed such horrors as crucifixion, flaying, an ingenious method of rending a man apart using bent saplings (fortunately none were at hand), but the lank-haired, evil-looking one named Fernando, who had something of his master about his grim visage, ended their talk by ordering them to prepare a fire beneath one of the pine trees.

While they began to build it, Dubois was manhandled over to a low hanging branch and strung up by his wrists, dangling in mid air while they piled the faggots beneath. In moments, the pain was excruciating and his arm sockets felt as if they were already aflame, but Fernando had more sauce to add to Dubois' torment.

'We will slow roast you Frenchman and your dying agonies will be like music to our ears. What do you think of that?'

For answer Dubois spat at him in his fury but missed and the wretch gave a sneer as the final kindling and shavings were placed around the base. Then, without so much as a pause, he struck a match and threw it into the pile.

Dubois has faced death a thousand times in a hundred different circumstances, but oh, it was most painful then – but not for himself you understand. All must die and this flesh is heir to decay and sorrow, but Dubois had at least hoped to make his end in battle on the field of honour. Yet this? His humiliating death would condemn Odette to that villain's perfidious clutches and it was almost more than Dubois could bear to think of. He began to shout and curse and scream at them incoherently, employing the rich vocabulary that only a seasoned trooper could muster. Yet his toes began to feel the first heat of the fire's embrace and as the flames licked ever higher, he tried rocking back and forth. But the motion sent spirals of agony racing up his arms, even though it brought some small relief from the gathering heat.

'Ha, we will have roast Frog tonight brothers, although this one doesn't look very tender.' They all laughed at his crass witticism but real fear began to build inside Dubois now. Do not believe any man who tells you they could face such a fate with equanimity. They are liars and Dubois is not ashamed to say he began to babble, imploring, praying, cursing, promising anything that would spare him this ignoble end.

Dubois' boots began to smoulder and even that slight heat was becoming unbearable as he swung back and forth over the central flame. Now he could only hope that it would be over quickly. The fire crackled and popped, slewing showers of sparks into the cold night air and the rope which bound Dubois' legs must have been aflame awhile as it snapped, leaving him bucking like a newborn colt. For one second Dubois' heart soared at this new found freedom, but his arms were still bound tight and it just bought more loud guffaws from his captors, who shouted vile encouragements and elbowed each other in their cruel delight.

'Dance the Flamenco next, Frenchman!'

But Dubois saved his breath and continued kicking to increase his swinging, for above their mocking he had heard something they had not, a distant, regular drumming which a born cavalryman recognises from the cradle. The pounding drew closer and now they heard it too, for they ran to snatch up their weapons and peered trembling into the night. Hoof beats! Hah, the sound of salvation! It must be a squadron at least as the clatter echoed around the trees and now they were almost upon us and these brigands were recoiling and running around like a pack of curs in their terror! The first horse burst into the clearing, a cloaked rider on an enormous roan and his lance buried itself deep into the chest of one of Da Foz's foremost men, impaling him to the trunk of a tree. A lancer! *Mon Dieu*, were our brave Polish allies to be Dubois' rescuers?

There was flash from the rider's sabre, Dubois' bonds parted and he hurtled earthward, more sparks flying as he danced daintily over the blaze. Dubois must confess it must have looked most comic, but he was in no mood for levity as he snatched up the fallen man's cudgel. The rider's pistol barked once, another brigand fell and Da Foz's men began showing their heels, scattering into the darkness. But the one called Fernando and two of his bigger ruffians were 'ow you say, made of sterner stuff and advanced upon Dubois, determined to finish the job. He prepared to defend himself, but his arms were still like knotted bundles from his painful suspension and desperately, he searched the trees for the rest of the horsemen to come to his rescue.

Yet now the chorus of sounds had disappeared and it was just that single rider who wheeled and came to his defence. Both of Fernando's henchmen turned to receive him and Dubois faced off against Da Foz's lieutenant with just a knobbly stick, which felt like shaking matchwood in his hands. He was a brute of a fellow too and came in swinging his crude sword like a scythe, as if he would beat Dubois down like a sheath of corn.

But the art of the true swordsman is not about strength, but finesse and timing and dancing back, Dubois gave ground, easily evading his clumsy blows. Fernando came on with another hefty swipe, over-balancing and this time Dubois' rapid riposte smashed into his wrist, forcing him to drop the weapon. The gnarled head of Dubois' cudgel came up, crunching into his jaw and as he staggered, another precise blow smashed into the back of his leg, forcing him onto his knees.

Nimbly, Dubois skipped around and kicked him in the back, which has the desired effect of plunging him face first into the blaze which was meant to consume this French 'ussar. Even though it does Dubois no credit he must confess, he planted a boot on the back of his neck and held it there while he screamed as if all the torments of hell had come upon him. Finally Dubois took pity and stoved in his skull. To this day he feels not the slightest 'int of remorse.

Meanwhile, Dubois' rescuer has dealt most skillfully with his opponents. One lay against the base of a tree, clutching his guts which another musket ball had blown open. The other lay wide eyed and dead, a tell tale sabre cut across his face. The pale rider walked his roan over slowly, sheathed his blade and dismounted quietly, offering his hand.

'Are you quite well, sir?' he asked in immaculate French, but from his dress and manner Dubois could tell he was not of our *armee*.

'A touch singed Monsieur, but fortunately mainly underdone thanks to your timely intervention… for which I offer you my eternal thanks,' Dubois replied in his passable *Anglais*.

'Pff, think nothing of it, it would be a black day indeed when I left an honest soldier, British or French, to the tender mercies of Da Foz's rogues.'

'You know that base villain then?'

'Oh, I do to my sorrow and have observed his activities with growing trepidation. He courts both sides in this conflict, playing each against the other for his own darker purposes. A most cruel and unnatural fellow is the Marquis.'

'Unnatural? I know nothing of that, Monsieur. My quarrel with him is entirely personal,' Dubois replied.

'Indeed?'

'This very night he has stolen the woman I love, tearing her away from her good father for his own depraved purposes. I was in pursuit when I was waylaid and overcome by his villains.'

'Forgive the indelicacy, but may I inquire as to the name of this young lady, Monsieur?'

'Why, it is the fair Odette, the only daughter of Colonel d'Hiver of the Guard.'

'Ha! So his greater design takes further shape, yet why would he…? It is strange, Da Foz is not normally distracted by the temptations of the flesh. So why kidnap this mademoiselle - saving your presence - no matter how lovely and why risk discovery with so transparent a crime? It is most unlike him, he must have another purpose.'

'If he 'as, I care not, for I intend now only to resume my mission and rescue my love.'

'Then I trust you will not object to some company, sir? It seems our purposes are as one in bringing Da Foz to justice.'

'If you would do me that 'onour, Monsieur, I would embrace it most heartily. If I do not mistake my guess, you are one of milor' Wellesley's 'Eyes'?'

'Indeed, but it is not on the Duke's business that I ride tonight, nor England's, but for another purpose. I have been watching Da Foz for many months now, observing, studying, waiting for him to make his move. And now I find he has struck impulsively, a course of action which is most unlike him, for normally he is the most patient and careful of men. Something has changed, something significant and it is – if you'll forgive me, sir – not just milady which has prompted him to take this action.'

'Whatever his motive, I will see Mademoiselle d'Hiver restored to her father, or die in the attempt and the devil take Da Foz!'

'Indeed, but I fear even the devil would think twice before supping with this blackguard. Come then, let's be about it.'

'Ah, but in all this confusion, I have clean forgotten my manners, Monsieur. I have the 'onour to be Lieutenant Gaston Dubois of the *Empereur*'s own 13th Death's Head Hussars. A pleasure to make your acquaintance...?' Dubois clicked his still smouldering heels and made an elaborate bow. 'The honour is mine, Lieutenant. Seraph is my name, Major Seraph.'

After Dubois' *petite* ordeal, he was glad to be back in the saddle of his beloved Rosalind and as we began to eat up the kilometres on Da Foz's trail, he regarded his new companion and ally from the corner of his eye. It was the work of moments to see he was no ordinary soldier, for he bore little of the manly aspect and bearing one would expect of the gallant gallopers, those dashing British officers who operated beyond the lines of the regular army.

Major Seraph sported no moustaches as Dubois had seen the brave British 'ussars wear and indeed his dress was most plain and sober, with nothing of the dash or panache one would expect of a *sabreur* of any nation. The buff coat and riding breeches were plain, unadorned by any braid or decoration and indeed, he foreswore even the Busby, seeming to prefer a most understated top 'at. Yet for all these evident defects in his attire, there was a certain stern calmness to his bearing and despite the rather weak chin and long, almost unseemly, pale hair and rather fey voice, his narrow eyes glowed with an intensity and otherworldliness, an *outré* quality, that spoke of steel and purpose. Nor could Dubois easily forget that he had acquitted himself most forcefully in the heat of battle and he was glad, yet also a little nervous, to have such an ally by his side.

We passed through dark, lavender scented woods and rode along the top of desolate ridges moving as fast as we could while following the trail, all the time straining to get a sighting of our quarry, but to little avail. Now, the air began to have a salt tang to it and suddenly, riding out of the dense darkness of the trees, a vast bay stretched out before us, the waves of the ocean shimmering in the moonlight.

Major Seraph reined in and produced a folding telescope from his pocket. 'There,' he pointed and Dubois could just see, across the curve of the bay, a small cloud of dust of the kind thrown up by a single horseman. For a moment he thought he glimpsed the retreating figure but then it was hidden by a hill and enveloped in shadow. Above, perched on a promontory, loomed the towers and ramparts of an ancient fortress, its crenellated walls and crumbling battlements speaking of an old, Moorish lineage. It was undoubtedly the domain of the *Portugais* nobleman, though Dubois 'esitated to 'onour him with such a title.

'So that's Da Foz's lair,' said the Major. 'That makes a lot of sense from what I know of the creature.'

'And what is that, sir? Is he then known for his seamanship?'

'In a manner of speaking Dubois, in a manner of speaking. Let's just say I suspect he may have more than a passing affinity for the ocean.'

'Pff, why should this concern us? Let us onward and storm this foul creature's castle. I am eager to be reunited with my love.'

'Steady, Lieutenant, I understand hussars are known for their bravery …and their impetuosity.'

'It is true, sir. We hold it a disgrace to live beyond the age of thirty.'

'Indeed? But this is no occasion for a full scale frontal assault, Dubois, not if you want your lady returned intact …and alive.'

'I want that more than life itself, sir.'

'Good then perhaps you'll rein in your natural instincts and heed my words. Da Foz is no mere aristocratic fop. He is a very dangerous…

man and here, on his home ground, even more so. We may face foes here, allies of his, who are more than shall we say *naturel.*'

'Sir, surely you are not in earnest? There is little room for such superstition in this age of reason.'

'Believe what you wish, Lieutenant, I only hope you are proved right. But come, let us reconnoitre further forward and seek an alternative way into Da Foz's den.'

We dismounted and the major attempted to stealthily remove some curious looking flasks from his saddlebags. They seemed to glow with a strange fiery light, but he did not deign to answer Dubois' quizzical eyebrow as to their contents. 'owever, after carefully muffling their hooves, we led our horses on a circuitous route along the cliff top of the bay. We wound over the rocky coastal paths taking care to remain out of view of the castle walls until we could conceivably lead them no further and then picketed the beasts in a small grove of stubbly trees. Rosalind was not *sanguine* and whickered most pitifully at the prospect, until Dubois nuzzled her head and breathed into her nose.

This done, the closer we got to the walls, the more the smell of the sea pervaded, but this was not the clean fresh tang of the ocean brine, but a foul, fishy stench, like the rotting of a shoal of fish guts. It made Dubois feel *tres mal,* but the major seemed quite immune from its formidable reek.

Now we moved forward like *tirelleurs* – pardon skirmishers – flitting from cover to cover and as we did so, Dubois took the opportunity to study the castle. With each step, the major's words seem to grow in *crédibilité,* for it was a sinister place, shrouded in dark shadows which seemed to absorb or perhaps deflect the clean beams of pure moonlight. In a great many places the walls were crumbling and tumbled down, as if assailed by the ages and its whole character spoke of *désordre,* neglect and perhaps something darker. Although Dubois could see no sentries, he had the distinct impression we were being watched from within, though *certainement,* any such observer would immediately have raised the alarm. Yet he could not dismiss the feeling and as we crept beneath the eaves of the walls, he found himself quite *craintif—pardon,* fearful – and immediately he had to draw upon all his reserves of manly courage to suppress a violent shudder.

'Shall we climb the walls, Major?' Dubois whispered, seeking to mask any craven thoughts with the certainty of action.

'Hm, I think ... perhaps not. If I'm not mistaken this small path may yield a more desirable mode of ingress, though perhaps… no, it is nothing. Come let's explore this way.'

THREE

The Sentinel on the Stair

The route the major had chosen wound down beside the walls towards the sea and each step was more terrible to Dubois than a direct assault upon the walls. Yet an 'ussar does not blanch or 'esitate and one thought of his poor Odette quite restored Dubois' fortitude. So he followed in the major's footsteps and kept one hand tightly gripped upon the 'ilt of his sabre. Down and down we went, the winding path becoming more slippery, flecked with moistness and spume. The smell grew bolder too, more intense, such that he was forced to press a perfumed handkerchief into service, lest he gag like an *enfant*.

The path stopped abruptly above a small but precipitous cliff over-looking the roots of the castle walls and there, surrounded by choking vegetation and salt-rank seaweed, was a small break in the rocks, a cavern entrance wreathed by the wisps and vapours of a sea fog. It was dark, black as a Cossack's soul and although Dubois had never been prone to the night terrors, the very sight of it quite unmanned him, or perhaps he just 'ad a foreboding of what was to come?

'We must pass through here, Lieutenant, I am afraid it is the only way,' whispered the major, striking a dark lantern under his cloak. 'Da Foz's men would have cut us down in an instant up there.'

'But I saw no-one.'

'Quite so, yet there they were. This way, though more perilous, will see us inside undetected.'

'More perilous?'

'I'm afraid so, there is no way to prepare you adequately for what we may encounter, Lieutenant. All I can say is stay close to me and trust in your courage. It is your best, perhaps your only hope.'

'My only? But Major…'

'Don't talk, just follow.'

The narrow beam of the major's dark light lit our way and inside we crept like mice in the wainscoting until the blackness quite swallowed us up. The walls ran with rivulets of moisture and Dubois took one last look back at the cave entrance behind him and the comforting sweep of the moonlight. This strange man's words had unnerved him more than any explicit warning might have done and again, he found his courage tested. Another thought puzzled him too. Even the mightiest of fortifications have concealed sally ports, yet with its commanding position and formidable walls why would the inhabitants of this castle leave this way open and unguarded?

True, it was well concealed and the major had sniffed it out like an 'ound upon the scent, but Dubois' misgivings would not so easily be dismissed and he tried to quell his beating pulse. Give him a sword in his hand and a clean fight and you would not have found Dubois wanting, but the dank eeriness of this place was hard even for the most fortitudinous soul to bear.

For it was also clear that this was not an entirely natural cave, but had been built on and enhanced by many hands over the long centuries. The ceiling was 'igh, strangely 'igher than any man might require and in places had been fashioned into arches which bore a strange geometry that hazarded the eye. Steps had been carved into the rock by unknown hands and their smoothness and great size made progress harder rather than easier, as if the way had been designed for giant rather than human feet. That awful fishy smell, which had been pungent enough outside 'ung like a discordant note in the air and added further to Dubois' apprehensions.

We had not travelled far, but already we must have passed under the castle walls and ahead, in the dim glow of the dark light, it was just possible to see this tunnel intersect another at right angles, one way sloping up, the other heading down. Suddenly the major stopped, stooping low and grabbed Dubois with a force which belied his rather slender frame, pulling him back into an alcove in the wall. There was just time to see his hand pressed against his lips before the shutter came down on the dark lantern and then we were pitched into utter blackness. Long moments, which seemed like minutes, passed as we crouched there in the darkness and Dubois was just on the point of whispering to the major when he heard it, a noise, distant at first but growing closer. Oh, *mon ami*, how to convey that awful, 'orrible, sinister sound to you, which would have frozen the very marrow of your bones?

It is strange to retell even now, but it had a kind of damp quality as if it had been hauled from the depths of the sea, and Dubois had the impression of something slippery passing over the rocks, but as if it were sucking at the stone. That smell returned, rising to such a pitch and intensity, that Dubois wondered he did not gag and retch. Then, even though he could see nothing, he had an impression, no more, of three large, terrible shadows, blacker portions of the blackness, crossing the space where the tunnels intersected. One of the shapes stopped and Dubois was quite unnerved and to his shame, cowered from its gaze, quite unmanned.

There were sounds, *Mon Dieu*, at once both alien and chilling, like no speech of this earth, like the ghost of a tide, the whisper of the sea. How he did not scream in his terror, to this day he does not know, but he felt as if his very soul were being torn and stretched by these unnatural shades. Then the shadow moved, passed and was gone, the wet squelching sounds receding as they, whatever *they* were, retreated down the tunnel. For long moments Dubois was simply too stunned to move or speak, until he felt the major's hand upon his arm.

'My compliments, Lieutenant,' Major Seraph whispered and as he turned Dubois seemed to see a strange light burning in his eyes, like the embers of a coal fire just before they are extinguished. 'Not many men would remain silent when confronted by such creatures,' he said.

'What were those things?'

'Fortunate for you, that you do not know. Suffice it to say that we have just encountered Da Foz's allies and let us leave it at that... for now. With any luck, you will not meet their like again and your life will be all the healthier and your mind all the saner for it. Now, let us journey onward before they return.'

The major unmasked 'is lantern and Dubois took a moment to collect himself, then followed as he turned right and up into the upper portion of the tunnel. We 'urried on, not daring to look backward or downward, where distantly Dubois could hear the waves crash with a peculiar violence against the shore.

Upward and ever upward we moved along a tunnel which had been made on the same gargantuan scale, but the more distance we put between ourselves and that intersection, the more Dubois liked it. After a while, his natural *virilité,* never easily suppressed, once again began to reassert itself and the 'ussar who feared not a mortal thing upon the face of this earth reintroduced himself.

Now we prowled under the foundations of the castle, along a path which showed the passage of the years, for the way was worn and smooth, as if many feet had walked here down the long ages. The major's lantern threw vast, elongated shadows upon the walls and Dubois began to see many strange pictures, reliefs and friezes which came from many different times and places. There were many *outré* geometric patterns after the Moorish fashion, which seemed to blend and whirl and fascinate the eye and occasionally, he would catch glimpses of some more modern depictions which seemed to show uncanny creatures emerging from the sea and walking upright upon the land. One of the Moorish designs in particular caught Dubois' eye and he found himself drawn to its sensuous gyrations. The pattern seemed to quite rob him of his will, drawing him into that shifting, opulent void, until he could have looked upon it for all the remaining days of his life. It was only the major's firm grip upon his shoulder that eventually broke its spell and returned him to his senses. The major quickly hurried Dubois onward before he could gaze upon it again, as every fibre of his soul begged him to do.

Now, a faint luminescence began to seep through from the end of the tunnel and Dubois could see a portal framed by the starlight. He hurried toward it, ready to escape the womb-like confines of the earth, breathe pure, clean air and feel the sweep of the skies above him once again. But the major held out a firm hand to arrest Dubois' progress.

'Not so eager, Lieutenant. The way ahead is barred.'

'I see nothing, Major, let us....'

'No, you do not see it, but there is something there nonetheless, a sentinel of some kind. I can sense it. Da Foz would not leave the entrance to his lair – even one so perilous to traverse as this – totally unguarded.'

'Ver' well, what do you propose?'

'Here, take the lantern a moment.'

The major reached into the folds of his cloak and removed and unfastened a rather plain looking sabretache. Then he began muttering under his breath as he nimbly sorted through the vials and jars and potions, eventually determining the one he needed. It was a small leather pouch and contained, as far as Dubois could see, a small heap of rather ordinary grey looking dust. The major sprinkled a portion onto his gauntlet with elaborate caution and then, eyes blazing again with that strange witch light, said simply.

'Lieutenant, I would advise you to look away now, for once seen, the thing revealed cannot be unseen. Yet if you do choose to behold it, you will gain a deeper understanding of the darker nature of the fabric of the universe we inhabit and your eyes will truly be opened to the threat Da Foz presents—albeit at some cost to your peace of mind. Know that I nor anyone else will think the less of you if you decline. The choice is yours.'

'...It is a strange dilemma you pose *un homme,* Monsieur. But lay on, Major, I am not afraid,' Dubois said with a bravery he did not entirely feel. But he had already allowed fear to govern him too many times that night and he was not ready to wilt again before the gaze of this stern Englishman.

'Very well then, stand back,' he said and with that breathed in, seeming to ingest lungfuls of air until he had drawn in many times what a normal man could hold. Then he pursed his thin lips and blew upon his palm, projecting the powder in a long, cone-like exhalation until it quite filled the doorway. At first the powder eddied and swirled, thick and choking, saturating the atmosphere with flecks like cinders. Then, as it began to settle, silver flakes glowed and glinted in the still night air, seeming to coalesce around a vaguely humanoid shape that barred the entrance. It was a vast being, the height of a man and half as much again and its limbs and body were bulky and weighty, silvery and scaled. At its neck, nebulous gills seemed to twitch with unclean life and its head and jaw were heavy, the nose multi-tentacled like the appendages of an octopus. Yet the true horror lay in the outlines of its eyes, which were cold and dead, containing a blackness like the stellar void.

Its form was ethereal and insubstantial like a ghost, the spectral outline of an aquatic demon, for such Dubois took it to be and indeed, it seemed it could be nothing else. Dubois, who had never doubted the sane and rational in his entire adult life, recoiled in horror, almost turning and fleeing from this apparition.

Yet the major did not tarry and was intoning strange words and phrases in a language Dubois could not understand. His fingers wove complex patterns in the air which seemed to leave an after image behind them, the multifarious trace of a five-pointed star hung there suspended. The effect upon the creature was remarkable; at first, its insubstantial frame shook with anger and rage and its facial tentacles writhed, quivering in agitation. Yet then it seemed to quail, retreating from the image as if –foul creature though it was – it were the one afeared. As the sigil faded, so too did the creature, slowly diminishing until it was just wisps and shreds of smoke and then they too were gone and only starlight remained.

'There,' said Major Seraph, 'our path is now quite safe. Are you ready, Lieutenant? I see you may have questions?'

'*Merde,* Major, where to begin? What mysteries, what sorcery is this, that flourishes in this age of reason?'

'A convenient label for a mere moment in the course of human history and that itself, a mere footnote in the wider history of the universe.'

'But this creature, what was it? And what did you do to it? How… why?'

'Perhaps it is not wise for you to dwell too long upon this, Lieutenant. Suffice it to say that being was a guardian, a sentinel conjured by Da Foz to bar the way into his fortress. As to my methods? Well, he is not the only man able to marshal extraordinary forces to his cause. Perhaps now you begin to apprehend the true purpose of my coming here? I'm sure milady d'Hiver is as precious to you as life itself, but Da Foz is no ordinary villain, but a creature who consorts with the demons of the sea and the powers of the outer dark. He must be stopped before his foul purpose, whatever that is, manifests itself.'

'At its neck, nebulous gills seemed to twitch with unclean life'

'*Incroyable*, if I had not seen, I would… I would call you a liar, a madman if you had asked me to believe in such things. Yet now I have the evidence of my own eyes. What are we to do, Major?'

'Let us move into the castle and find Da Foz's lair, but quietly, Dubois, we would do well not to give any signal of our approach.'

'Rely on my discretion, Major,' Dubois said, running a finger down the edge of his blade.

FOUR

The Call of the Ocean

The portal led out to a shadowed corner of the courtyard and we took advantage of the darkness to allow our eyes to adjust and survey the inner workings of Da Foz's den. Major Seraph was right to preach caution, for upon the crumbling ramparts could be seen several of the Marquis' ruffians covering the approach to the walls. To attempt them would have been a short road to a ball through the 'ead or a sword through the throat. Yet the way he had chosen was scarcely less perilous and Dubois was still reeling inwardly from what he had seen. Yet amongst the many follies of youth, one of its few virtues is an ability to focus on the immediate. So, rapidly dismissing any thought of supernatural terrors, Dubois quickly scouted the courtyard, searching for a way to proceed.

Far above, in the inner keep, was the *donjon,* the fortified great hall which formed the inner sanctum of any such fortification and it was there Dubois knew we must find the Marquis. The major was of a similar mind for he indicated a set of lighted windows near its top.

A quick nod of agreement and we were on our way, seeping through the shadows, dark shades ourselves, clinging to the patches of gloom which seemed to breed within those walls. Through the courtyard we snuck our way, pausing to allow two degenerate looking hirelings to saunter past on their patrol, then secreting ourselves behind some barrels at the bottom of a stone stair. Dubois was all for a swift dash to attempt the battlements but the major stayed his hand and it was just as well, for above we heard in broken *Portugais*.

'What are the master's orders?'

'Keep a weather eye out. Fernando has not returned and he thinks one of the Frogs may come in pursuit. Yet none have attempted the walls.'

'Perhaps they have found the hidden way?'

'Pff, If they have, they'll wish for a swift ball through their brains or their throats cleanly slit. For the sentinel does not feast upon flesh alone, but it will crack their marrow before devouring their very souls.'

'And the others?'

'Will be up at high tide. Come, we have much to prepare, while the master entertains himself with the wench.'

The iniquitous cackle which greeted this foul observation almost caused Dubois to leap out and strike them down in blood and fury, and the quiet way be damned! *Tres fort!* But the major's wiser head and iron-like grip prevailed and with some difficulty, Dubois kept his peace until their footsteps faded away. But murder was in his heart now and woe betide any of Da Foz's *suppôts* who crossed his path!

Onward we crept up the inside of the stair and onto the battlements where Dubois could hear the sea lashing against the rocks below. The major led the way with seemingly unerring instinct as we slipped through a small portico and into a side door which led into the main body of the keep. As he fastened the portal quietly behind us, the major unshuttered his dark light again and we found ourselves in a dusty, long abandoned corridor.

Now we were inside the inner defences of this foulest of creatures and we began to move upward, ever upward, flitting from cover to cover and 'astily concealing ourselves whenever the servants of Da Foz made themselves apparent. In any great campaign or battle, surprise is one of the most useful allies of all and suspecting nothing of our intrusion, the creature's minions went about their business with apparent unconcern. Dubois could not help but notice that like the brigands who had ambushed him earlier, they were an ill-favoured crew and here, away from the gaze of the outside world, their cold, bulging eyes, pallid skins and *poisson*-like features were even more pronounced. Dubois wrinkled his nose in silent contempt at these degenerate specimens. What exactly was Da Foz the master of here?

To add to his disgust, the very castle walls emanated an oppressive atmosphere, seeming to speak of centuries of neglect with their dingy, shadowed 'allways, rotting tapestries, rusted weapons and decaying suits of armour. That putrid, fishy smell, though not as strong as in the tunnels, seemed to permeate everywhere, assaulting the nostrils, numbing the senses and provoking a primitive, instinctual revulsion that was distinctly unsettling.

Yet, despite these distractions, we kept our course true and managed to gain the upper stories of the keep without any misadventure. Our path brought us up a final set of stone steps to a wide landing. Here at least, some attempt had been made to preserve the values and refinements of normal civilisation and society. This open space was much cleaner, 'ung with newer arras and lit with fresh torches, revealing portraits of what could only be Da Foz's ancestors set against the designs of the original Moorish walls.

Dubois was certain that the 'eavy, ornately carved wooden door must lead to Da Foz's chambers, a fact confirmed by the presence of several armed thugs lounging in front of it. So he whispered urgently, 'Come, Major, time and Odette's honour are of the essence! Let us put these beasts to the sword and then swiftly deal with their master.'

'Lieutenant, please do try and at least contain your rasher impulses. Da Foz must have no warning of our coming'

'*Mais* 'ow then, Major? There is no way to dispose of these thugs so swiftly that we will make no noise.'

'No natural way, but lend me a few moment's patience and I will see what I can conjure.'

The major rummaged in his sabretache and extracted what looked like a small, azure jewel which glowed with inner fire.

'Now, Lieutenant,' he whispered, 'as soon as the jewel ruptures, waste not a moment but have at them. Use sword, pistol, whichever you prefer, both if you must, but know we have exactly one minute's grace before this will help no more. Make sure the business is done by then.'

'But Major...'

'A pistol ball took the first one through the eye'

'Ready?' he said and Dubois nodded, not quite comprehending, but trusting that the major knew his trade. With that, he lobbed the brilliantly coloured gem into the middle of the stone flags where it shattered into dozens of multi-faceted shards. Dubois did not know what to expect, an explosion or something combustible possibly, but that was the sum of it, no more, no less and suddenly the major had leapt out to engage Da Foz's men directly. A pistol ball took the first one through the eye, the flash and powder blinding and acrid in that enclosed space and the major's next shot took another clean through the throat. That one fell clutching his neck, blood drenching the floor.

Not to be outdone in valour by an Englishman (no matter 'ow gifted), Dubois was at his heels, pistol in one hand, sabre in the other. Often, in the heat of battle, time seems to pause, slow and curl in upon itself and one sees with such clarity, that each second lasts a lifetime as each successive move in the tableaux is played out: sword against sword, blade versus blade, stroke matching stroke. Yet as he rushed forward,

31

steadied his hand, fired and another ruffian fell, some part of his brain was screaming that something was dreadfully amiss.

There was little time to consider it then though, for now there were just two of Da Foz's rogues left and we must press them 'ard to take advantage of this apparent minute's grace. The major took the smaller fellow, while Dubois engaged a great bearded rogue who came swinging a wicked, curved scimitar that must have last been employed in anger in the *Reconquista*.

He dealt Dubois a great lusty blow so that his sabre shivered as he parried and the deflected stroke cut through a corner of his Busby. Dubois' involuntary reaction was a hearty '*Merde*!' which he exclaimed loudly and at the top of his lungs, but the curious thing was he 'eard… nothing. Neither his words, nor the clash of steel, nor now he thought of it the discharge of our pistols had made even the slightest of sounds.

As a quicksilver repost cut his lumbering opponent down, Dubois saw that the major was also laying on his strokes – but again in total silence. Major Seraph was a skilled swordsman, but perhaps lacked a touch of the martial strength we 'ussars value so highly and as he locked blades with his ruffian, an underhand elbow knocked him back, dislodging something from within the folds of his cloak. For a moment his gaze was fatally divided, then *sacre blue!* He dived to clutch the object mere centimetres from the flagged floor. This laid him wide open to the villain's sword and as the moustachioed lout pulled back for a vicious overhead cut, which surely would have made an end of the major, Dubois was forced to intervene.

Dubois' blade caught his edge the breadth of a whisker away from the major's forehead and then a whirlwind of cuts forced the *Portugais* to fall back and let us just say, soon he troubled us no more. As Dubois wiped his blade clean, he saw the major hastily conceal the object back within his cloak, but despite his precautions, he readily recognised it as one of the glowing flasks he had seen him remove from his sabretache earlier.

Curious, but Dubois had no time to dwell upon it, for the remainder of Da Foz's villains lay around us, dead or dying. The major went from each to each, checking for signs of life and extinguishing it if he found any. Dubois made to protest, for this was surely not chivalrous behaviour, even for such a debased foe, but the words found no substance as they left his mouth. It was as if he had been struck dumb and rendered voiceless.

The last rogue expired in silence just as the last points of light from the major's jewel winked out and as they did, the ordinary background hum of life returned.

Quietly the major remarked, 'I know, Lieutenant, it seems harsh, ignoble even, to treat such a downed, helpless foe thus, but it is necessary I'm afraid. It is imperative that Da Foz knows nothing of our approach. Quite simply, I could not take the chance.'

'But that bauble, how does it confer such silence? With such a device, one could do anything. Ambush battalions, surprise armies, cut the throats of generals… why, even Empereurs would not lie safe in their beds!'

'Handy little trinket isn't it? But don't worry, it doesn't work for longer than a minute or on any such grand scale and I would have no use for such a device in the normal course of human affairs. Yet when one encounters the darkest magic, one must oppose it with all the tools at one's disposal…'

'True, I suppose, Major,' though the pricking of Dubois' soul was not entirely in agreement with his words.

'And what of this flask? Was it so precious that you would gamble your life for it?'

'Oh yes, Dubois. That precious and perhaps more so.' The major, possibly sensing Dubois' disquiet at his rather maladroit evasion, said quickly, 'Now, let's see about this door.'

Instinctively Dubois reached for the wrought iron handle, but the major 'ow you say, wagged his finger. 'Perhaps best if you allow me, I have a feeling this is no ordinary entranceway.'

While Dubois took the opportunity to reload his pistols, Major Seraph inspected the door looking it up and down, intently scrutinising each element of its composition. At one point he even sniffed at it! The door was old, the dark stained wood worn over the centuries, its intricate carvings faded by the rigours of time. It must surely have come from the Moorish era of the castle's occupation.

Major Seraph touched but did not turn the handle, then he raised a sceptical eyebrow and desisted from trying the lock at all. Instead, his fingers traced their way across the flowing patterns and then his gloved hand hovered over the points of a faded star near the top hinge. He pressed each of the points of the star lightly, there was a barely audible click and then the portal swung open gently. The major motioned with a finger placed over his lips, then insinuated himself inside, beckoning Dubois to follow.

Da Foz's bed chamber was fashioned like the inside of some oriental potentate's seraglio. Lofted, delicately arched columns divided the room into a series of smaller spaces and it was richly decorated, with many fine pieces of dark wooden furniture, ornate room dividers, opulent hangings and plush, richly patterned carpets. The room contrasted with the shabby, faded state of the rest of the castle and evidently its master revelled in the taste, elegance and a certain sensuous luxuriousness that he denied his brutish followers. Here no fishy odours lingered but instead a warm, sweet, 'eavy scent pervaded the air, spreading an ardent, drowsiness as if desire itself had been made flesh.

Low, sensuous music played like the piping of many flutes or a chorus of ethereal otherworldly voices, though Dubois could detect no source and the music seemed conjured from the very air itself. It leant the scene a most disturbing, salacious, erotically-charged air.

On one wall a large open fire burned away in its hearth, lending the space a sultry warmth and as we flitted from pillar to pillar, its flames seemed to flaunt themselves brazenly, throwing dancing shadows across the ceiling. At the furthest wall was a grand four-poster bed and there, strewn amongst the sumptuous, scattered pillows and cushions, in a state of partial *deshabillement* was the pale form of Odette! Dubois' first instinct was to dash to her at once, but remembering the major's words, he 'eeded his warning and stayed his hand.

On the opposite side of the chamber, was a large table stuffed with all manner of esoteric arcana, like the explosion of an alchemist's laboratory. Ancient, weathered tomes lay in stacks on its surface and by its feet and on the wall behind were pinned up many maps and manuscripts, scrawled with strange symbols and glyphs which Dubois could not discern with any clarity. Many of them carried motifs and pictures drawn from the sea and there were more disturbing images too which showed beings emerging from the waves, terrible things, like the strange offspring of man and fish that made the hairs on the back of Dubois' neck stand to *attention*. And there, poring over a book bound in a strange pale leather, was Da Foz himself, sat like a lobster over its supper, one eye hugely magnified through a set of nested lenses. Dubois' thumb slipped easily upon the hammer of his pistol.

'Pah, the *Cthaat Aquadingen,* such a crude translation from the Middle English, wouldn't you agree? Come sir, step out into the light, don't be shy,' the creature said in a half-mocking tone without bothering to look up from his work. At this, the major subtly signalled Dubois to stay hidden and boldly stepped out.

'Ah, Major Seraph, of course, I thought it must be you, for indeed, who else could it be?'

'Who else indeed, Da Foz? You know why I am here.'

'Of course, but it will avail you little.' Silently, Dubois worked his way around to one side of the pillar and sighted the length of the barrel down his arm at the scoundrel's body.

'And Lieutenant Dubois too? Ah, I am doubly blessed, but please no need for such toys, Gaston.' Da Foz made some strange gesture with his hand, which caused Dubois' eyes to recoil and suddenly his pistol seemed to squirm and twist in his grasp as if it were possessed. Throwing the cursed weapon to one side, Dubois half drew his sabre and prepared to meet the villain with cold steel.

'Stay your hand, Lieutenant,' said the major. 'I am curious to hear what the Marquis has to say. For if there is one thing I have learned about his kind, it's that they can never resist a chance to boast of their nefarious designs.'

'Indeed? You are too kind, *Senhor* and well, I am flattered naturally, for your name is spoken of with the highest respect in the circles I keep. Respect and not a little fear, I might add.' Da Foz laid off his study of the object beneath his lens and stood up to address us both.

'I am glad to hear it,' said Major Seraph, nodding with a most super-cilious incline of his forehead, 'Though perhaps, Da Foz, you would satisfy my curiosity on one point?'

'Please, ask away,' said the Marquis.

'Why the girl? Why reveal yourself by such an action? Surely you must have known you would be pursued? That this would provide just the pretext I needed to hunt you down? Why would a creature of your inclinations have any use for a mortal maid?'

'Oh, you mistake me, sir. Oh, I am certain, saving your presence, Lieutenant, the fragrant Odette would breed me many fine sons. But forgive me, it is almost laughable to suppose I would have risked so much just for the daughter of a mere colonel, whatever her more... obvious charms. No, no, you quite mistake me, sir, it is not *la donzela* I sought, not *la donzela*, but her treasures.'

'What?!' Dubois interjected. 'But she has no treasure, no dowry, her father is an honest man, but poor...'

'Oh, but she has, Lieutenant, though not one that many ordinary men would recognise, perhaps. Indeed you were close to them all night and your breath must have caressed their very surface, yet you saw them not.'

'You speak in riddles, villain...'

'Then let me bring... enlightenment. And with that Da Foz lifted Odette's necklace up into the light. The dark smoky stones glinted in the firelight and seemed to dance with an interior light that Dubois had not seen before. Da Foz cradled them and his eyes glittered with avarice.

'For this trinket, this bauble you have abducted her, insulted her, made a mortal enemy of me?' Dubois exclaimed.

'Oh, please, have no concern for your *amour* Lieutenant, her virtue remains intact, I assure you. She is a charming young woman, yes, but such are common enough. No, what I find extraordinary is how one such as she came into possession of these stones.'

'I have no idea, her father mentioned they had been in the family for generations. But this is absurd, you kidnap her, attempt to murder me, for mere stones? Why, they are not even diamonds.'

'Not even diamonds? Pff, you have no conception of their true value, their true power, do you Dubois? I should have known, hussars have the intellect of a carthorse and the instincts of a donkey, but the Major sees, the Major knows, do you not, *Senhor* Seraph?'

'But this is extraordinary,' said the major and momentarily, even his impassive features dissolved into an expression of perturbation.

'Surely these cannot be those fabled Crystals of Hydra, thought lost and passed beyond the knowledge of mortal man for millennia?'

'Ah, but they are Major, they are. Yes, yes, even you feel their pull and now you begin to understand why I risked all. Time passes swiftly on the surface, but oh so slowly beneath the waves and we have not forgotten what was once ours. Can you imagine, can you even conceive of how I felt when I glimpsed them around the delectable neck of Mademoiselle d'Hiver?'

'I believe I do.'

'How they fell into her possession after all these long centuries, I do not know and I do not care. But it was all I could do not to snatch them away in an instant, even without the churlish threats of our rash Lieutenant here. But my will cannot be resisted and now these crystals will once again reside in the hands of their rightful owners.'

'He babbles Major, let me run him through,' Dubois said. 'We will revive my beloved, return her jewellery and be gone…'

'I wish it were gibberish, Lieutenant, but I rather fear the Marquis speaks the truth and this is a much graver matter than I first suspected. Many thousands of years ago, when the isles of Atlantis reared their spires against the primordial skies, the first men fought a great war against the sea demons, beings from the depths of the ocean, the so-called Deep Ones. The conflict raged for decades, centuries, until a great sorcerer rose among the Atlanteans. He is said to have stormed one of the Deep One's most sacred temples and succeeded in capturing one of the sources of their power, a vast alien crystal which he shattered into many shards. It is fragments of these lost shards that appear to form Mademoiselle's necklace.

'The story is widely held to be legend and has only come down to us in whispers, rumours in some of the darker, more forbidden tomes of ancient times,' continued the major. 'No one has seen an actual piece for centuries. To discover an entire set, why, it's almost inconceivable.'

'Inconceivable, yet surely you believe the evidence of your own senses, Major?' said Da Foz suddenly stalking across the room and holding them up to the fire. 'See, see how the waves dance in their opaque depths. How can you doubt it is so? And if that were not proof enough, I feel them, I feel the tingle of their magic through my fingers, I feel it coursing through my veins. I think you sense it too. Oh, have no doubt, Major, these are indeed how you English say, the genuine article.'

'And what do you propose to do with these lost treasures?'

'Do Major? Why restore them to their rightful owners of course.'

'Monster,' Dubois said. 'Even if we suppose all this were true, why would you side with these creatures, these Deep Ones, against your own kind?'

'Oh, but we are not his kind are we, Da Foz?' said the major. 'For he is one of them, unless I mistake my guess. Note the pallid hue of the skin, the strange cast of his eyes, the Marquis is one of their foul spawn, part human, part demon.'

'You see much, Major,' said Da Foz, inclining his head mockingly. 'Your reputation is apparently well deserved. You are perceptive to name me their offspring, though I prefer the term 'hybrid', a composite being who combines the strengths of both species.'

'Or their worst vices.'

'Naturally I prefer to look upon it in a more positive fashion, but yes, I cannot deny I hear the call of the deep, for I have already bathed in the currents and tides and frolicked in the ocean's garden. It will not be long before the call becomes irresistible and I will descend and return to the surface no more. But what a gift I will bring to pave my way to immortality. I will be the one who restores our ancient power and banishes the depravations of man.'

'The depravations of man?' said the major.

'Yes, the depravations!' he spat. 'For even now my brothers and sisters have noted how mankind begins to grope his way toward enlightenment and the first stirrings of the industrial age. In under a hundred years you have harnessed the power of steam and tamed the forging of iron and steel. The smoke from your factories belches into the sky and heralds the dawn of a new age, when your machines will allow you to spread across the surface of the world like a canker. I will convince my brethren that we must not allow it.'

'And how will you stop us?'

'Oh, very good Major, allow me to prattle on so I reveal my plan to you, making it all the easier to thwart I suppose. But no, I rather think that this time, I will leave you in suspense.'

'Leave us where you wish, villain,' Dubois said, having subtly manoeuvred himself closer while the beast raved. 'For you will never leave this place alive!' And with that Dubois slashed at his throat meaning to carve a crimson streak there.

But the villain was quick, as quick as any man, quick in a way that was not quite natural and he ducked under Dubois' blow, slid aside like quicksilver and stabbed at a portion of the mantelpiece. To our amazement, the whole stone fireplace suddenly rotated, like it was on oiled hinges, taking Da Foz with it and then he was gone, secreted safely on the other side. There was a sound behind us and where Dubois' darling Odette had lain just moments before, now there was just an empty space on the bed.

'Rash, Lieutenant, very rash!' said the major with some irritation, rapidly patting the mantelpiece where Da Foz must have depressed a secret switch.

'Don't waste your time, Major,' said Da Foz. 'It is a one-way mechanism which quite seals the chamber. The Moorish architect was indeed a cunning fellow and most thorough. Don't worry, Lieutenant, I will take the utmost care of Mademoiselle d'Hiver. Now, perhaps I can continue my oration without further interruption, for there is no earthly chance of your escape.

'A keen student of ancient lore such as yourself, Major, will know that my brethren have many cities and dwellings spread across the depths of the ocean floor, indeed, even the crude scholar who translated the *Cthaat Aquadingen*, supposed as much. Yet we are still very much at the mercy of distance: time and tide and all the natural hazards of the oceans. It was not always thus, for in ancient times, before that cursed Atlantean interfered, the power of the crystals allowed us to open up a secret pathway, to travel almost instantaneously across the void, ignoring the perils of topography and the expanses between our mansions.

'These fragments will allow us to span those deeps once again, uniting our scattered colonies in a way that has not been possible for millennia. We know that these crystals seem to speak to each other and with the correct rituals we will be able to trace even more if any survive. That will allow us to link our ancient dwelling places until we dominate the land as well as the sea once again. Then the paltry industrial might of man will avail him not, for the new dominion of the Deep Ones will begin!'

'Never,' said the major quietly.

''Never' in this case will be a very short time, Major, for the hour approaches when I must again convene with my brethren and give them these glad tidings. Say your second and final farewell to the mademoiselle, Lieutenant, for neither of you will leave this room alive. As for you, Major, it has been neither an honour nor a privilege, yet I would have expected rather more from a man of your reputed talents. No matter, for I see you are quite disappointingly mortal after all. Farewell then, perhaps you should be glad you will not live to see it, for the conquest and enslavement of mankind is likely to be a most protracted, not to say painful process.'

The villain's footsteps echoed down some hidden stairway, but his taunts lingered in the air along with their import. Dubois looked to the major, but he seemed lost in thought, yet we were not spared in our deliberations for long, for almost immediately there was a noise from beyond and a low, seething hiss began to fill the chamber. For a moment Dubois was at a loss to explain it, then he saw the heavy, smoky vapour which was seeping through vents in the bottom of the walls. It curled and writhed insidiously over the floor and one small breath of that foul, noxious odour was enough for Dubois to determine that Da Foz was not flooding the room with expensive cologne.

The major was already tearing at the bed sheets making makeshift masks to wrap around our faces. Dubois hammered at the door where we had entered, while the major tried the mantelpiece once again, but both were in vain. The room was sealed tight as a drum head.

As we hastily donned our improvised masks, the vapour swirled around our feet and ankles, slowly climbing toward our knees, but Major Seraph's voice was calm and deliberate as he ordered, 'The gas is heavier than the air, we must seek higher ground, quick up, up on the bed.' We leapt onto the mattress of the four poster as the gas tip-toed ever upward, its vile curls and twists eddying like malignant fingers. Perhaps we only delayed the inevitable, but what else could we do? One fights for every last second of life when one is 'ard pressed.

Merde but our situation was desperate and in that moment Dubois would gladly have faced a dozen of Da Foz's thugs, that strange, unquiet sentinel or even those loathsome unseen creatures from the passageway, rather than succumb to this creeping death. Despite his many fine qualities, an 'ussar is made for action not cogitation and Dubois could see no way out of our current predicament. Surely we were not to die here, caught like vermin in Da Foz's foul snare?

'Major?' he enquired and could not entirely keep the tremor out of his voice as the vapours began to seep upward, washing over the mattress, onto the covers and curling around our boots.

'There must be a venting mechanism, something so that he can return to the chamber unharmed...' the major muttered to himself. 'But where to find it? Not in the room for certain. Well, desperate times call for desperate measures... Lieutenant Dubois, I will trouble you to face away from me.'

'You have an idea?'

'Perhaps, but under no circumstances and I mean *no circumstances*, no matter what you hear, must you turn around. Do I have your word?'

'*Oui*, Major, *oui*, anything.'

'Very well, look away Dubois, quickly now, if you please.'

Dubois did as he was bid, turning so that he faced outward. The deadly fog was rising higher, up to his waist now. Whatever the major's plan, he would need to enact it at the *chargez*!

Then, from behind Dubois heard strange sounds, guttural words, incantations, *stranger* phrases that seemed to have no right to exist in the human tongue. There was a flashing of light in colours that he had never seen before or since, there was a retort like a *blancmange* being sucked through a whisk and it was only with the greatest difficulty, he restrained himself from turning to see whatever strange business the major was transacting.

Yet Dubois had given his word and an 'ussar's word is not for breaking even though the vile vapours continued to rise, swirling above Dubois' chest, insinuating their way up toward his neck.

In spite of Dubois' vow, he must turn to seek higher ground or be engulfed by those vile mists, yet when he did, he saw nothing but the vapours, the major was gone! He had vanished like a wayward priest's conscience when he views a comely maiden. Cursing through the mask, Dubois leapt upon the dresser and scrambled up to the topmost canopy of the bed. He was in shock… surely his comrade would not have abandoned him to so *terrible* a fate? Yet where was he and more importantly, how had he made his escape?

Reaching higher ground, Dubois shouted, 'Major! Major Seraph!' But answer came there none and as the deadly fog continued to rise, the vapours crept over the edge of the canopy, oozing and percolating through the cloth. Dubois raised his head to the highest extremity he could until it scraped the stone ceiling. Then he held his breath like a drowning man does against the tide and as the first tendrils began to twirl over his moustaches and seep through the cloth, the acrid scent penetrated his nostrils and he coughed and gagged. His last thoughts were of his poor, lost Odette and he knew that if we would meet again, it could only be in eternity.

It is said fate, *destinée,* is inexorable, but Dubois believes it can be cheated or at least held at bay by certain gifted fellows and the major was one such, *un homme extraordinaire* who could twist and bend it to his will, as the blacksmith works the molten steel. For, just at the final moment, when Dubois believed he could hold no more air in his lungs, there was a great wrenching, a sucking sound and then strong currents of clean air blew from below, filling the chamber and causing the deadly miasma to dissipate. *Merde*, but Dubois had never smelled anything so sweet in his life! It was a close run thing, for another breath or so and all would have been done.

Dubois exhaled a great gasping sigh, spluttering from the small amount of noxious fumes he had inhaled but quickly scampered to the lip of the canopy to discover his means of deliverance. There, wedging a makeshift stopper into an expanse of a semi-revolved fireplace was Major Seraph, who greeted him cordially.

'Ah, Lieutenant, there you are, I am glad to see the venting mechanism worked promptly and my actions were not too tardy. How are you feeling?'

'As if I had smoked a thousand cheroots and inhaled the discharge of the entire grand imperial battery, but I am still here Major, which is more than I could have 'oped mere moments ago…'

'Good, good. Well, look lively, come down and give me a hand with this will you?'

Dubois scrambled down from the arras and helped the major wedge a pole axe into the mechanical device which allowed the fireplace to revolve.

'But how did you escape the chamber? 'ow did you pass beyond the wall? 'ow did you find the means to save me?' he asked as we gave the poleaxe a last heave into position, snapping the head into its gears, so it was jammed *ouvrir*.

'It is probably best that you don't peer too closely into my methods, Lieutenant. Shall we just say they are not readily explicable to the man of reason and leave it at that?'

'Ver' well, if you insist Major, I will not press you further, let me simply offer my thanks for my own unworthy 'ide.'

'Not strictly necessary old boy, but you're welcome, nonetheless. Besides, our work here is not by any means done and I could and would not abandon so dauntless a comrade.'

'Da Foz…' Dubois said and his eyes narrowed at the mere mention of that villain's name.

'Indeed, I believe the perfidious Marquis means to enact his ignoble plan tonight and while breath remains in my body, I mean to stop him. How are you, Dubois?'

'A little dizzy, that is all Major, but eager to land a blow on that villain and restore *mon amour*.'

'You'll do then. Come, I don't believe we have much time.'

FIVE

The Bridging of the Void

Scarcely pausing to gather weapons and snatch a lantern to light the way, we were soon proceeding down the hidden passage where Da Foz had made his cowardly retreat.

The narrow stone stair wound down through the vitals of the castle, twisting into its very core and in this 'idden space, its occupiers had not bothered to hide their affiliation with the dark. Strange, other-worldly motifs and reliefs spattered the walls, showing men worshipping things from beneath the sea, bowing down before them. Dozens of more horrible, unmentionable scenes were also illustrated, including some which featured diabolic orgies and unnatural congress with these beasts. Dubois shuddered and tried to keep his eyes averted from such depravity, instead keeping a tight grip on his pistols and his feet at the double behind the major's.

But what would we find at the end of this passage? Despite Dubois' own uncanny experiences earlier and these horrible works of 'art', he could still barely credit Da Foz's assertion about this undersea race who needed Odette's jewels to – what was it? Project themselves across the abyss? It seemed insane, inconceivable, far easier to dismiss him as an utter madman. Yet if one thing leant it credibility, then it was the major's absolutely ironclad certainty about this *incroyable* tale. He was no *naïf* – and that is perhaps what unsettled Dubois most of all.

As we descended into the bowels of the castle, the light from Dubois' lantern scarcely seemed to illuminate the walls at all, as if it were being absorbed by the darkness, but that foetid, fishy smell began to assert itself once again. Lower now and as the stone steps finally began to run out and give way to more natural formations, Dubois could hear the sound of waves lapping and breaking against the rock – and close by too. Then the steps came to an end and the rough floor and walls of a natural cavern disappeared off into the dark.

'That lantern will warn them of our coming, best extinguish it, Dubois.'

'But 'ow will we find our way?'

'Don't worry, I was born part feline, just grasp the end of my scabbard, follow close by and watch your step. These rocks are slippery.'

Deploying what Dubois believe you *Anglais* call *haussement d'épaules Gallique*, or what we French simply call 'a shrug' to display his insouciance, Dubois did as he was bid. Slowly, we crept through the dark, Dubois' left hand grasping the major's sword casing, the right groping ahead of him so he would not falter. We moved on like *deux souris aveugles,* pardon... two blind mice, but the major seemed to indeed have the vision of *une chat* and although that rotten smell and the misgivings of Dubois' own querulous 'eart caused him no little dismay, onward we continued to press.

Fortunately, it was not long before a faint light began to trickle through from the way ahead and Dubois was able to leave off trusting to his guide's surefootedness and begin to make his own way.

Now, Dubois could hear the sea resounding as it crashed against the rock and the salt of the surf hung 'eavy in the air, as we inched along the last few metres of passageway and concealed ourselves behind a small outcrop of rock.

From our vantage point, Dubois could now see into what looked like a huge natural stone cavern. Furthest away from us, to seaward, a great aperture opened in the rock to admit the waves, which washed into a saltwater pool foaming across the floor of the cave. Great stalactites 'ung down from the ceiling of this sinister place and they had been carved, brutalised almost, into twisted unnatural pillars and arcane forms that gave the scene a most ill-starred air.

At the landward end, the rock had been hewn into a huge altar and looming over it were two enormous statues, vast loathsome amphibious monsters in 'umanoid form. The quality of the workmanship was unnerving, for it picked out fine details on their scaly skins, rippling gills, savage crests and webbed limbs that gave them a hideous, realistic quality, such that you would swear that at any moment they might spring to horrible, ghastly life.

The remainder of the cavern was comprised of many tiered terraces and galleries like honeycombs through the rock and now, pouring through them, a foul congregation began to assemble, as if summoned by some silent signal. Da Foz's followers were an *hétéroclite famille, pardon,* a diverse group, comprising those muscular villains who guarded his castle, some degenerate looking peasants and even a few deserters from the *Armee Iberian* and milor' Wellington's ranks, judging by the ragged remains of their uniforms.

As they shuffled in and took their places, Dubois' attention was drawn to the altar itself and the most singular object which dominated it. There, inside a weighty frame fashioned from some unearthly glittering metal was what looked like a great polished mirror, though no reflection played upon its mirrored surface. Its irregular shape was decorated with the treasures of the deep and at each point of the compass from north, all the way around to north north west, was placed a socket shaped like the fronds of an anemone. It was a most alien and disturbing object and although the mirrored surface was opaque, it seemed to pull the mind toward it and scatter one's senses in many directions. It was only with a supreme effort of will, that Dubois managed to avert his gaze from its siren-like hold.

Once the last members of that vile coven had taken their places, a quiet descended over their unholy ranks and even the sound of the waves seemed to fall into an ominous silence. Suddenly the air was rent by a singular voice

'Father Dagon! Mother Hydra, hear me!' Da Foz stood next to the mirror, his voice echoing back from the walls and as one, his flock turned their gaze toward him, their breath an echoing sibilance, like a whisper of the deep. He wore a cloak of lustrous, dripping seaweed, interwoven with vile ocean flowers, a crown formed of the spines and claws of *les fruits de mer* and in his hands he clutched a twisted, barnacled trident, like an 'orrible parody of Neptune. His eyes brimmed with fervour as his voice reverberated.

'By the waxing of the moon and the rising of the tide, your servant calls, let the sound echo from deep to deep. Let your family, once more, be complete!' With this he struck the mirror-like object a resounding blow which caused it to ring out in a single, atonal note which carried across the water. At this, the congregation turned its gaze seaward.

At first, nothing much disturbed the surface of the water but then, it was as if the very motion of the waves paused, frozen in a moment. Ripples and bubbles began to appear in the water as *they* began to emerge from the tidal wash. The moon was behind them at first, making silhouettes of the abhorrent heads and crests which broke through the waves. Bulging, piscine eyes glowed with a terrible malevolent phosphorescence and their gill sacks heaved and rasped as they tasted earthly air. They stood upright now, hulking bodies tipped with scales and ridges, the grey-green of their flesh contrasting sharply with the pallid white flabbiness of their bellies. There were perhaps fifteen of the creatures and their webbed, amorphous limbs brought them to a halt on the edges of the pool, where they stared up at Da Foz in silent, terrible communion, smaller reflections of the vast effigies above. As one, their mouths opened and a terrible croaking emerged, like the high pitched squabbling of a flock of diabolical gulls.

'Deep Ones,' whispered the major, but his chilling observation was interrupted by the sound of Da Foz's greeting.

'Welcome brothers and sisters, welcome! Now we are assembled and the family of the ocean assembled.' Da Foz scanned the cavern and his voice rose and now swelled with triumph.

'You come to us my brothers and sisters when the moon is full and the tide is high and you arrive at the cusp of a new age, a new era when the tyranny of mankind will be overthrown.' Da Foz held up Odette's smoky jewels which brought an audible chittering from the horrible conclave below.

'Yes brothers and sisters, yes,' continued Da Foz. 'That which was thought to have been lost forever has been found! The forgotten pieces gathered! The ancient pathways may be reopened!'

Now the creature's high-pitched squawks became even more animated and murmurs echoed and spread amongst the ranks of the human congregation.

'Ripples and bubbles began to appear in the water as they *began to emerge from the tidal wash.'*

'Bring her!' shouted Da Foz and two hefty henchmen appeared from the wings carrying a forlorn looking Odette between their greasy paws. Dubois cursed loudly, but fortunately the sound was swallowed up by the excitement of the crowd.

'Steady, Lieutenant,' hissed Major Seraph.

'But what shall we do, Major? I will die before I let them…'

'Stay calm and be ready, Dubois, I just need a moment…' While the major cogitated, Dubois eased a pistol from his belt and loosened his sabre in its scabbard. The henchmen were chaining Odette to the upright slab behind the altar now and the sight made Dubois' blood boil and his moustaches quiver. Pffaw! Futile or not, at that moment he cared little for his own life and he was quite ready to rush the altar and die with his sword in his hand defending his beloved from their vile depredations. Damn their eyes, he would make sure these vile beasts remembered the name of Dubois to their dying day.

'For mankind waxes strong!' screeched Da Foz. 'His smoke pollutes the skies, his dyes run into the rivers and his effluent begins to pour into mother ocean. Unchecked, his machines will ravage the earth, poison the seas and he will spread like a plague across the face of the waters. He must be curtailed, brought to heel, contained. It is time to re-establish the natural hegemony of the Deep Ones, time to restore our ancient byways, time to re-open the crystal void! Tonight, Mother Hydra and Father Dagon will be our witnesses!'

'Damn it, this is worse than I imagined. He means to summon the Deep One's rulers to put the seal upon his infamy,' said the major. 'This changes the complexion of things somewhat.'

'I know nothing of complexions, major, but I do know my Odette lies trussed and upright there like *une poulet* in a butcher's window.'

'Just give me a few more moments, Dubois.'

'*Dépêchez-vous* Major, for I will not suffer to witness this for long.' Dubois glanced back to where Da Foz continued his oration.

'…for mankind's transgressions are plentiful, his sins against the bountiful seas legion and his jealous eyes covet our ancient treasures. Even now, his envious spies lurk amongst us! Seize him!'

Suddenly Dubois was aware of them, burly arms reaching out to take hold of him and his sabre whirled, carving a crimson arc through the air. A limb flashed, he parried a blow from a cudgel, skewered one of the ruffians *en point,* but an 'ussar's blade is made for cutting not thrusting and as he tried to withdraw, the metal turned and lodged in the fellow's guts, causing him to howl. Dubois levelled his pistol to take a shot at the sea of faces, but then a cruel blow caught his wrist, the pistol dropped, they swarmed all over him and he was wrestled to the ground.

Blows rained upon Dubois until he thought he must lose his senses and then, abruptly he was dragged upright. Futilely, he attempted to shake off his captors, but his arms were gripped firmly by many hands and he was dragged and hauled along the galleries and up to the dais.

There Da Foz's mocking eyes greeted him, a sardonic smile playing about his lips and just as Dubois' vision began to clear, he was forcefully bound upright alongside his *amour*. Odette bravely whispered 'Gaston' and both relief and terror were there in her face. '*Courage mon amour*' Dubois mouthed back, but where our salvation was to come from, he could not say.

'I am surprised to see you, Lieutenant, alive at least,' leered Da Foz. 'How is that possible I wonder? The Major's magics must be more formidable than I supposed.' Suddenly Dubois realised he and Odette were up here alone. Where was Major Seraph? Dubois had not been aware of him during the brief fight; had his comrade deserted him... again?

Balefully Dubois gazed at his tormentor and at that moment it was not death he feared, but the humiliation of dying without a sabre in his hands and a curse on his lips.

'The Major *est mort*,' Dubois sneered. 'He succeeded in springing your trap, but succumbed to your vile poisons. I will mourn my lost comrade later, but unchain me now you hound and by god...'

'Not by your god, Lieutenant, he has no place here in the womb of Mother Hydra.'

Weak though Dubois was, he strained against his bonds, dying to free himself and land at least one blow on the villain's visage. But it was no use, Dubois was bound fast and all his efforts were to no avail. Da Foz merely laughed and leered and took up the stones, dangling them mockingly in front of Dubois. He began mumbling an incantation and words which were not words came tumbling from that twisted mouth, the spell growing louder and louder until it echoed the speech of the creatures below. They in turn responded, emitting high pitched clacks and chirrups, their excitement and agitation growing and the chanting grew louder, taken up in a horrible chorus by the human worshippers, until the atonal dirge swelled and boomed, filling the cavern. Then, when the cacophony was at its zenith and Dubois could swear his eardrums must shatter, Da Foz raised his arms above his head and the place fell to a sudden silence.

'Let the oldest ties be renewed!' shrieked Da Foz and carefully, methodically, he began to place a smoky jewel in each of the mirror's sockets. As he went around its face, each of the small fissures opened, expanding like a flower toward the sun and then gave a small sigh, as tiny, anemone-like tentacles grasped each stone and pulled it into place.

'Let the ancient avenues be restored!' Now that all but the topmost stone had been positioned, small rivulets and streams of bright water light began to flow between them.

'Let the void… be opened!' said Da Foz, placing the last stone and then the circle was complete. For long moments nothing happened, then a change began to come over the mirror, the solid surface turning liquid, rippling with small waves, as if it were subject to the pull of time and tide. Unholy dark light played around the portal and then a watery image began to form inside, slowly resolving into a coral dais which overlooked the peaks and spires of a vast underwater city, one populated solely by the same creatures which lurked at the tide line below! *Mon Dieu* it was horrible, yet strangely fascinating to see those demons in that vast alien vista.

Da Foz's worshippers watched too, a collective moan issuing from them as they beheld the change. Dubois looked around desperately, wracking his poor brain to formulate a plan of escape, yet his bonds held tight as ever and this poor 'ussar could see no means of escaping his fate.

'Yes, brothers and sisters, the way is open and soon we will rejoin our family as we step through to greet our brethren beneath the waves. I will summon Father Dagon and Mother Hydra and receive their blessing for this hallowed endeavour.'

At this the congregation gave up a strange keening and the creatures below began to take up a new chant, one that was rich and guttural, laden with sinister cadences. Da Foz began tracing strange paths and movements through the air and even though Dubois' eyes could scarce credit it, he could swear his hands left a faint afterglow so that the symbols seemed to linger for a moment, horrid import contained in their unholy patterns. Now Da Foz's voice joined the 'orrible cacophony of man and creature, but it took on a more urgent, insistent, beckoning quality, as if he were calling someone or indeed, *something*.

Far out to sea, huge spouts of water suddenly erupted from the ocean's surface and the waves began to rage and swell, resolving themselves into two gigantic plumes which began to move ominously toward us. The dirge grew and swelled and Dubois cursed he had not the liberty of his hands to stop up his ears, for he felt he must go mad with the sound of it. Da Foz's speech rose octaves and his voice seemed to enter a pitch which had no natural place on this earth. As the spell reached its climax, the two plumes began to charge and race and surge toward the shore, swelling and dancing until they dominated the whole horizon, like shadows filling the sky. Da Foz now pushed his face mere inches away from Dubois' own.

'You first, Dubois, then the girl!' He spat. 'Your blood shall usher in a new age, the end of man and the beginning of the supremacy of the sea!' He returned to that vile alien language to complete his incantation, drew back his trident for the thrust and Dubois braced himself to receive the killing blow...

But suddenly that cruel face was enveloped in flame, his voice transforming into screeches of agony as fire played 'orribly around his features! The chant died, the trident tumbled and Da Foz staggered away as he desperately tried to beat out the flames which began to engulf him. With the invocation interrupted, out to sea, the giant waves faltered and subsided, their peaks diminishing, petering out, until they became just a succession of white plumed rollers, which broke placidly towards the shore.

Dubois wrenched his head around to see what miracle had intervened to save us and there, *sacre blue!* who should it be, but the major himself?

Yet this was not the fey, rather *outré* British army officer who had first accompanied Dubois on this night's dark adventure, but a vengeful archangel, wreathed in a shroud of smoke and flame! A fiery cloak adorned his shoulders, burning fiercely, flame writhed and twisted over his body and Dubois swears he hovered a metre above the ground rather than walked upon it. Those pale, unblinking eyes had been transformed into fiery coals wreathed in sulphur and brimstone, which seemed to have been drawn from the lake of Gehenna itself. Flame played about his face and head, a halo of fire, although strangely, it seemed not to consume his flesh. On either side, he was flanked by two glowing *efrits*, strange female creatures of light and flame drawn from the fable of a Thousand and One Nights, blazing like miniature suns orbiting around him.

For a moment Dubois was rendered speechless by this apparition, as, it seemed, were the unholy congregation around him and the only sound was Da Foz's scream as he plunged and fell from the dais into the water below. Seraph, or this fiery vision of him, regarded the scene for a moment and then stretched out a finger, like Da Vinci's creator reaching to Adam, and with a blazing smile playing across his lips said, 'Allow me, Dubois.'

Liquid fire arced from his fingers, searing Dubois' bonds which dropped smouldering to the floor and it was the work of seconds to retrieve his weapons, then position himself to protect his darling. Dubois was ready, eager even, for any onslaught from the sea demons or Da Foz's degenerate minions, yet he could have saved himself the trouble, for Major Seraph and his flaming houris chose that moment to begin their assault, laying about them with flaming vengeance.

The major extended his arms and sent a series of fireballs careering into the galleries and colonnades of that unholy temple. Where they landed, they flared, exploding with a deadly force, charring flesh, singeing hair and scattering Da Foz's human disciples. With shouts of dismay and cries of terror they left that place far more quickly than they had entered, beating and trampling each other in their panic to escape from the major's searing retribution. *Mon brave,* it was a stirring sight, the Empereur's own artillery could have done no better and it was with much joy Dubois watched those foul worshipers beat a headlong retreat with 'ow you say, their tails between their legs.

As for the sea demons, well, at the major's unspoken command, the *efrits* began to engage them, hurling cascades of fire which rained down into the shallow pool where the Deep Ones still stood with their fishy eyes and gaping jaws. One had the presence of mind to hurl a trident at the *efrits,* but the weapon charred and melted as it touched the djinn's molten skin and that seemed enough for those sea-born horrors. With a great hue and cry they turned tail and fled, diving back into the water in a maelstrom of scaly skins and thrashing limbs, until they were quite swallowed up by the waves.

The unequal contest may have lasted moments or minutes, Dubois could not tell, for he stood shielding his darling, but also gazing in awe at the fearsome havoc the major had wrought. It was truly a wonder, the major wielded the power of flame and hurled thunderbolts as if he had personal command of a more potent version of those absurd Congreve rockets, which we 'ussars frankly consider are only good for scaring donkeys, peasants and small children.

As the last of Da Foz's disciples disappeared off howling into the night, the major floated down onto the dais. With a delicate bow he saluted the returning *efrits*, those strange denizens of fire and they acknowledged him too, returning the salutation. Then, they seemed to turn inside out and be sucked back in upon themselves, diminishing from fire to smoke, from flame to ashes, and then they vanished too, leaving behind just the faintest trace of brimstone. Dubois watched with fascination as the major's fire-shroud seemed to burn itself out, the flames smouldering and sputtering, until it too was just a faint outline and then it too was extinguished. The last thing to vanish was the fire in his eyes and he allowed himself a small smile at what must have been a look of utter astonishment upon Dubois' face. But in a moment, that expression of amusement had turned into a shouted warning,

'Dubois, look out!'

Dubois' blade whirled in a defensive motion and his instincts served him well, for his parry just caught and locked the points of the trident which had been spearing towards his vitals. Da Foz, his skin raw and blistered, had been transformed into an awful, ghastly, crisped thing and this blackened shade spat malevolently at Dubois as he tried to wrench back his weapon. But he was too slow and Dubois' own backhanded slash cut it from his fingers and those fingers clean from his hand. His curse lingered for a moment on the air, before Dubois' sabre took out his throat and he died gagging and frothing on his own blood, a fitting end for that despicable creature.

'Nicely done, *mon brave,* and I would say that concludes our business here, ' said the major as Dubois began to sever the bonds which still secured his beloved.

'Perhaps for you, Major, but I will not forget this night so easily, nor will my sweet Odette.'

'Nor should you my dear Dubois, but I hope that its conclusion proves satisfactory for both you and your mademoiselle.' At this he bowed gallantly to Dubois' dearest one, who, freed from her bonds, was now crushing him with her embrace, smothering him in a welter of kisses and innumerable, 'Oh Gastons!' Dubois must confess, he found it most gratifying.

'Apologies, *mes amis,* that I appeared to desert you, but I had to await the critical moment, when the final opening of the crystal void exposed both Da Foz and his creatures. I'm sorry that you had to play the unwitting role of bait upon the hook.'

'I understand, Major, *les moyens justifient les extrémités,* the means justify the ends. Please, think nothing of it.'

'But how did you know what would defeat him?'

'Elemental my dear Dubois,' the major smiled. 'It is said the best way to fight fire is with fire, but naturally it also follows that the best way to fight water is also with fire.'

'…and this magic you employ, those demons, the *efrit?*'

'Creatures of darkness, like Da Foz, are not the only ones who can draw upon the elemental forces of the universe to do their bidding. As for the *efrit* as you call them? Well, I carried them with me within those two jewelled cases for just such a purpose. They scarcely needed any encouragement, for even without my enchantments, beings of fire are naturally opposed to those of water. I had a feeling they might come in handy.'

'So the matter is concluded then and I may return my poor Odette home?'

'Very nearly, Lieutenant,' said the major as he reached over to where the surface of the great mirror churned and thrashed like the waves in a storm. On the other side, great legions of those creatures seemed to have gathered and they swarmed malevolently in vast shoals, some even darting toward the mirror's surface, before veering off at the very last moment.

'That's quite enough of that, thank you,' said the major as he deftly plucked out each smoky jewel from its socket. Almost instantly, the surface of the mirror calmed, faded and then resumed its former opacity.

'Stand back, if you please,' said the major and when we had retreated a sufficient distance, he sent a searing bolt of flame straight at the mirror's surround, melting it until it was just so much blackened slag.

'Now that, I very much hope, is the end of that.'

'*Mon Dieu*, so that is it? Victory? Da Foz and his evil are no more?'

'For the here and now, yes, but the struggle continues. There are always those who would harness dark powers, mingle their blood and make unholy pacts with beings from the depths. Yet, fortunately, there are also always brave men willing to oppose them.' The major nodded in Dubois' direction and Dubois found himself experiencing *le rouge au front*, 'ow you say the reddening of the cheeks.

'You are too kind, Major, but my assistance was hardly crucial.'

'On the contrary, Dubois, it was invaluable. Without your distrac… aid I would never have had the time to complete the magics which ultimately defeated Da Foz and his allies. Alas, I'm afraid I won't be able to return mademoiselle's jewels, these must be taken and hidden far beyond the reach of the Deep Ones' allies. However, I'm sure a representative sample from Da Foz's accumulated treasures upstairs will provide more than adequate recompense. They should be more than sufficient to set up a young, newly engaged couple for life; a life which I'm certain will be both long, fruitful and full of great joy. Come, *mes amis*, let us be away from this dark place and return to the clean night air.'

***

And so we made our way back up into the now abandoned castle itself and indeed most, if not all of what the major predicted came to pass, for he had an uncanny ability to part the veil of the future, that man. Dubois and his darling Odette were indeed eventually wedded (although that is an extraordinary tale in itself) and although Dubois continued to follow his beloved Empereur, until all came to an end on that *terrible* day in the muddy fields of Belgium, he defied the ordained fate of the 'ussar and lived to enjoy a long and prosperous life. Using Da Foz's treasures, Odette and Dubois eventually secured a beautiful, thriving stud farm in his beloved Ardennes where we bred *exceptionnel chevaux* from his beloved mares Rosalind and Eleanor.

As for the major? Well, that was just the first of our many great and *étrange* adventures together, indeed, it was the first time Dubois' eyes were opened to the many weird, supernatural forces which hover on the fringes of our understanding and which menace and threaten the stability of our world. It was on that day that Dubois first began to march towards his own peculiar and unusual destiny.

Many times we would encounter each other again and in the normal course of events this is how it would proceed. Quite unexpectedly the major would turn up with a cheery, 'Ah, there you are, Dubois, the very man I was hoping to bump into. Now, if you can spare me a few moments, there is a small matter I wish to lay before you.'

And so we would begin again.

But as for the further telling of those tales, Monsieur? Well, perhaps they are best left to another day. Come see Dubois again once he has rested and his wits are restored, for the recall of even such a mildly taxing affair has sapped his diminishing reserves, even if they have done his poor old heart some good.

And when you do best ask *mon patron* to secure us several more bottles. And we had best make them of the *supérieur* variety too, if you would be so kind, for Dubois will require much additional fortification to sustain him through the telling of his subsequent escapades.'

Dubois' adventures continue in
The Feast of the Dead

JOIN THE BATTLE AGAINST THE DEADLY MENACE OF THE MYTHOS!

Delve into the thrilling Mon Dieu Cthulhu! universe and join French hussar Gaston Dubois as he begins an epic journey in the fight against the powers of darkness!

Head over to www.john-houlihan.net and sign up for the newsletter to receive a free bonus story which reveals more about this exciting world.

You'll also get updates on new work including the forthcoming Keeper of the Hidden Flame, an epic new adventure where Gaston Dubois is inducted into a secret society who have long guarded humanity against the malign influence of the mythos and the powers of the dark.

There's also regular freebies, giveaways and competitions and a chance to shape the Mon Dieu Cthulhu! universe itself, plus a chance to participate in the development of the forthcoming tabletop roleplaying game!

MON DIEU CTHULHU!
Swashbuckling supernatural adventure!

<u>The Crystal Void Illustrated Version</u>

The year is 1810 and as Napoleon's marshals chase Wellington's expeditionary force through Spain to the lines of Torres Verdras, dashing if rather dim French Hussar Gaston Dubois is astonished to encounter the love of his life.

But the fragrant Odette is abducted before Dubois can consummate his passion by the Marquis Da Foz, a ruthless and sadistic Portuguese nobleman. The hot blooded Hussar is soon in deadly pursuit, but can he evade the Marquis' myriad traps and who is the mysterious ally, Major Seraph, who comes to his aid?

What strange horrors lurk within the shadows of the ancient Moorish fortress where Odette is held captive? Can the heroic duo foil Da Foz's dark machinations, defeat his unnatural allies, rescue Odette and prevent the opening of the dreaded Crystal Void, before it unleashes a new reign of terror on the world?

"Great story, interesting characters, lots of sword and musket action, and the potential for future stories in an underutilised setting."
– Sci-fi and Fantasy Reviewer

Feast of the Dead

It is late 1810 and as autumn turns to winter, Napoleon's Armee Iberian settles down to its siege of Wellington's "accursed earthworks" at Torres Vedras. Dashing French Lieutenant, Gaston Dubois, is given his first independent command: leading a detachment of hussars those "thieves on horseback" into the Spanish interior, in search of intelligence, supplies and plunder.

After a bloody skirmish, Dubois and his men take refuge at the Monasterio de St Cloud, an ancient ruin standing at the crossroads of this war-torn land, which now serves as a field hospital to soldiers of all nations. There, he encounters the unworldly Doctor Malfeas and the beautiful but fierce Mademoiselle Brockenhurst, who seem to offer temporary respite from the horrors of war.

Yet this former house of the holy holds many strange secrets and Dubois faces fresh battles on all fronts. In his own ranks against the surly Sergeant Sacleaux, his disgraced second-in-command, and externally, by a hostile countryside where every hand is turned against him. Yet most sinister of all is the malevolent mystery which lies at the heart of the Monasterio itself, an ancient and terrible enigma which threatens both the lives and souls of all who encounter it.

Alone, deep behind enemy lines and beset on all sides, will Dubois survive his first real command and can he prevent the horrible unravelling of the mysterious feast of the dead?

"An epic, swashbuckling Napoleonic adventure expertly blended with chilling Lovecraftian horror. One of the most accomplished, entertaining and quietly chilling Horror novels that I've come across in my dive into the genre." – Sci-fi and Fantasy Reviewer

"Highly entertaining, mixing history and fantasy for great adventures ...fall in love with Dubois and his inimitable style." – Egretia.com

Shadow of the Serpent

As the year 1810 wanes, dashing hussar Lieutenant Gaston Dubois finds himself at a crossroads. Following a duel over a crime passionnel, he is banished from his beloved 13th Death's Head Hussars and dispatched in disgrace to the "Accursed" 31st Dragoons

Placed in command of the unruly Second Company in a posting far from the glory and honour he craves, Dubois faces a series of challenges in his first formal command. Can he transform his dispirited men into an effective fighting force, prove his ability to command, and escape the murderous attentions of an odious fellow officer?

But even in this forgotten corner of the war, the forces of mythos and mystery are never far away. Dubois' duel was fought against no mortal man and he is plagued by uncanny events, a countryside hostile to the French occupiers and the wrath of a fearsome guerilla bandita, La Espina, who seems determined to have his head.

Called to arms in a decisive battle against the Spanish army, can Dubois and his company perform in the heat of battle, lead them to victory and restore his reputation and his honour?

THE SERAPH CHRONICLES
One man defies the might of dread Cthulhu!

The Trellborg Monstrosities

It is 1943 and the war hangs on a knife edge. Set free by a leading Nazi occultist, an ancient evil stirs in the snowy fastnesses of the Norwegian border, threatening to unleash an ancient artefact which could not only alter the course of the war, but the fate of humanity itself.

Hope though endures, as a band of brave resistance fighters and a crack team of British special forces combine to plunge deep behind enemy lines to confront this ancient horror. Yet is their strange civilian adviser, the mysterious Mister Seraph, truly on the side of the angels or pursuing some dark agenda of his own? Can the fearful Trellborg terror even be defeated by mere mortal men?

"A wonderfully evocative tale of blood, bullets and ice." – David J Rodger

The Crystal Void

The year is 1810 and as Napoleon's marshals chase Wellington's expeditionary force through Spain to the lines of Torres Verdras, dashing if rather dim French Hussar Gaston Dubois is astonished to encounter the love of his life.

But the fragrant Odette is abducted before Dubois can consummate his passion by the Marquis Da Foz, a ruthless and sadistic Portuguese nobleman. The hot blooded Hussar is soon in deadly pursuit, but can he evade the Marquis' myriad traps and who is the mysterious ally, Major Seraph, who comes to his aid?

What strange horrors lurk within the shadows of the ancient Moorish fortress where Odette is held captive? Can the heroic duo foil Da Foz's dark machinations, defeat his unnatural allies, rescue Odette and prevent the opening of the dreaded Crystal Void, before it unleashes a new reign of terror on the world?

"Great story, interesting characters, lots of sword and musket action, and the potential for future stories in an underutilised setting."
– Sci-fi and Fantasy Reviewer

Tomb of the Aeons

'The sands of the desert seem as unchanging as the aeons, but they constantly shift reform and remake themselves, so that one is always looking at a frozen moment in perpetual chaos.' – Commander Siegfried

It is 1941 and as Ernst Rommel, the Desert Fox, swings his great armoured right hook to send the British Eighth Army scurrying back toward Egypt, the crew of Ingrid, a mark IV panzer pursue a lone British tank into the deep wastes, only to be ambushed and knocked out.

When they awake, Ingrid's commander Siegfried and his surviving crew begin the long weary trudge back to their own lines, but soon become lost in an unnatural sand storm which seems to blow up from nowhere. When they stumble upon a strange temple complex and find a unit of dead Black Sun SS, they are forced to penetrate deep into the heart of the unholy ziggurat and recover a lost artefact, the Fangs of Set, by their guide and fellow captive Captain Seraph. Will they defeat this charnel house's newly awoken inhabitants and can they survive the horror lurking at the very centre of this tomb of the aeons?

"Indiana Jones meets HP Lovecraft" – Monty Burnham

"The writing is excellent and the atmosphere well-maintained ... it deserves to be widely read." – Sci-fi and Fantasy Reviewer

<u>Before the Flood</u>

The year is 2034 and Britain is a drowning isle, after a cataclysmic wave destroyed her cities, killing millions, raising the sea level by 60 metres and changing the landscape forever.

The Flood has brought Albion to her knees and now the Devils, a race of malevolent sea creatures, haunt her coasts as the survivors retreat inland, struggling for their very existence.

Mankind learns to fear the sea and avoid the water.

Then a mysterious island surfaces off the coast of Wales, a small team of British militia under the command of the war weary veteran Sergeant Emma Stokes, is dispatched to investigate this new threat. But a chance meeting with the mysterious Major Seraph takes them on a dangerous odyssey through this drowned world, to the hidden fortress-city of Gwaelod, which seems to offer new hope in the battle against the creatures. Yet as humanity clutches on by its fingertips, who are the real enemies in this deadly flooded world?

"The shape of water was not a love story, it was a warning."
Amazon Reviewer

"A cracking story. Pick up Before The Flood and devour it, then go onto the rest of the Seraph Chronicles. You'll be in for a hell of a ride!" -
Sci-fi and Fantasy Reviewer

SCIENCE FICTION

<u>The Constellation of Alarion and Other Stories</u>

Best Short Fiction Nominee British Science Fiction Association 2021

Ten insightful science fiction tales from one of British sci-fi and fantasy's most intriguing authors.

John Houlihan is best known for his Cthulhu mythos and historical fantasy series, but this is his first major collection of sci-fi stories, including debut play, Bomber Command.

In Most Exalted, the hero of the seven systems now resides in retirement, but when a series of suspicious deaths rock his veterans' home, will his dubious past finally catch up with him?

In Charioteer, countries settle disputes the old fashioned way, trial by combat. As the eve of a great contest draws close, will Soola finally step out of her brother's shadow and embrace her true destiny?

In the Constellation of Alarion, a fabulous treasure lies hidden in the midst of a deadly labyrinth. Can three galaxy-hopping rogues overcome the maze's lethal traps and their own bumbling inadequacies to claim it?

Explore ten tantalising tales and take a glimpse into a beguiling sci-fi future from one of fantastic fiction's most fascinating talents.

"A masterful collection" Sci-Fi and Fantasy Reviewer

Dark Tales from the Secret War

Dark Tales is a collection of 13 stories set in Modiphius' Achtung! Cthulhu universe, a world which mixes the terrors of HP Lovecraft's Cthulhu mythos with mankind's darkest yet finest hour, the Second World War. Thirteen unhallowed stories await within its covers, which range from the wilds of the South Pacific to the dark depths of the Black Forest, to the icy wastes of Norway. Edited by John Houlihan they come from a stellar cast of writers including David J Rodger, Martin Korda, Richard Dansky and the unsettling mind of horror master Patrick Garratt.

Expanding and exploring the Achtung! Cthulhu universe in bold, new narrative ways, these are the darkest of tales from the Secret War and feature the nefarious Black Sun, Nachtwolfe and their Nazi masters and the heroic Allied forces of Section M and Majestic, as well as many thrilling standalone adventures.

Dark Tales is available from Modiphius.net